inally, a novel for women and men...

THE
OVECOMMITMENT.COM

DOC SCRIVEN

ove is no longer a game, it's a science.

Insight Fiction

This is a work of fiction. The events and characters described herein are imaginary and are not intended to refer to specific places or living persons. The opinions expressed in this manuscript are solely the opinions of the author and do not represent the opinions or thoughts of the publisher. The author has represented and warranted full ownership and/or legal right to publish all the materials in this book.

Insight Fiction

ISBN: 978-0-9827432-1-8

PRINTED IN THE UNITED STATES OF AMERICA

To our grandparents, Elton and Ruby Edwards:
65 years of marriage and **T**he **L**ove **C**ommitment is still going strong.

Other Books By Doc Scriven

The Document: A Novel

How To Be A Better Man In 21 Days Or Less!

Acknowledgements

Fiction is not make-believe. In fact, fiction is where we often see for the first time what is and what can be. *TheLoveCommitment.com* is more than a novel, it's an experience. And a work like this could not exist without the shared experience of many. For this I must thank **T**he **L**ove **C**ommitment focus groups that met in Atlanta, Georgia and Baton Rouge, Louisiana for opening their minds, hearts, and lives to this project. I also must thank my inner core of readers (Amy Palmer Laster, Rashim Cannad, and Denice Myers) for giving me insightful feedback to improve the writing and clarify the concepts you will soon encounter. But I have to shout out my main man, Leman Raphael, for candidly giving his time to our frequent (often daily) conversations to create, understand, and properly express **T**he **L**ove **C**ommitment system. And to Latricia, who has been my **TLC** for the past 14 years and shaped much of what is written here. I have found more joy with you than I've ever known, and more love with you than I ever could have imagined.

Doc Scriven
August 2011

FACT: In 2008, 29% of White babies, 53% of Hispanic babies, and 72% of Black babies were born to **single mothers** in the United States.

TIME Magazine & the Pew Charitable Trust Survey, 2010

FACT: In 2008, 9% of Whites, 25% of Hispanics, and 26% of Blacks lived below the **poverty line**.

U.S. Census Bureau, 2008-2009

FACT: In 2010, the United States population was 72% White, 16% Hispanic, and 12% Black. However, of its 2.1 million **prisoners**, 34% were White, 20% were Hispanic, and 40% were Black.

U.S. Census Bureau and U.S. Bureau of Justice Statistics, 2010

FACT: In 2008, 56% of Whites, 50% of Hispanics, and 32% of Black adults in the United States were **married**.

U.S. Census Bureau, 2008-2009

FACT: In 2008, 44% of Black Americans polled said that marriage is **obsolete and unnecessary**.

TIME Magazine & the Pew Charitable Trust Survey, 2010

But What Are The Facts Really Saying?

Chapter One

Gigi

I'm so tired of dealing with trifling men. Can't walk two steps without them hounding you, but when its commitment time, they're sprinting away faster than Usain Bolt running from the LAPD. Almost need to hire Kojak, Columbo, *and* Inspector Gadget just to hunt 'em down. Take Timo for instance.

Timo was a stock broker with Merrill Lynch who wore $800 suits and smelled like Obsession. He didn't bathe in it. Only a hint; just like I like it. Timo took me dancing and to romantic dinners on the regular. Needless to say he was chocolate brown with rock-hard abs and enough charm to make a bald woman toss her wig in the air at a weave convention. That brother was 'foyn', you hear me? But when I asked him where things were headed between us one night while we were in bed, he started stuttering like Porky Pig, and things went downhill from there.

"Look, I'm not ready for a progressive relationship right now. I told you that when we met."

My eyes widened. "You're not ready for a progressive relationship?" I rose up from the pillow on haunches, incredulous. "You seemed to be pretty progressive twenty minutes ago while we were having *relations*." I looked him up and down. "So I'm good enough for you to lie between my legs, but not good enough to be your wife?"

Timo glanced from side to side and held up his hand. "Wife? Hold up. Who said anything about getting married? I thought we were two grown folks having some grown folks fun."

Timo flashed the smile that usually disarmed my pouting defenses. Not this time. I wanted to scratch some Nigerian tribal marks onto his face, but I didn't. You would've been proud of me. Kept it real lady-like. I decided to take the informational approach. So I softened my expression and went in.

"Timo, I'm 25 years old, Boo. My biological clock is ticking and it's not slowing down. I want to be married and have kids that I'm young enough to enjoy."

Timo recoiled, snatching the covers and wrapping himself in the sheets. "Kids? I know you're not pregnant? See, I knew I should've listened to Ricky and left you alone last year. He told me you had that 'setup' look in your eyes but I didn't believe him. Now you're trying to hang a baby around my neck? How do I even know it's mine?"

I hopped off the side of the bed, all five foot five inches of me standing there glistening…and glaring. "I've given you three years of my life and you have the nerve to accuse me of setting you up? How dare you? Tell you what. First off, I'm not pregnant. But I know that's your little defense mechanism kicking in to justify you running off into the night. Secondly, I make more money than you. So I don't need 'ann-nee-thing' you have. And lastly, raise up out of my bed, get your clothes, and go find another little girl to play house with…because you're about to get the hell up out of mine!"

The next time I saw Timo was three years later. The night I was out with Kenny.

Chapter Two

Gigi

Now before I get too far ahead, let me introduce myself. My name is Giovanni. Really it's Giovanni Nicole George, after Nikki Giovanni, but my family and friends call me Gigi. I insist that my men call me Giovanni because we're not friends. Instead our interactions are well defined and structured so there are no misunderstandings. You know, like a contract. That's so nobody gets led on or hurt or thinks something that's not spelled out, in black and white, by the other person in the relationship.

I also sell houses for a living. I don't show houses, I list houses. The other agents can run around trying to please buyers who often can't even buy. I simply wait to hear those four magic words whenever my phone rings: "I'm faxing the contract". If the other agent isn't saying that, there's nothing to talk about.

I sell upper end homes mostly. Last year I cleared about a hundred thousand after taxes and it's been like that for the past three. Certain zip codes don't have recessions. In fact, the worse the market, the more some people buy.

My clientele frequent charity events and political fundraisers. Generally people with extra cash are the ones giving it away to avoid paying taxes on it. So I just follow the tax breaks and, inevitably, I find the money. All I do is make conversation, casually tell people about my profession, and contact them a week or so after the event. Works like a charm.

Calls come in left and right from people who want me to list their homes for all sorts of reasons. Some couples want to trade up to something bigger or downsize because they're empty nesters. Other times, people call me when they're divorcing and need to sell the house quickly. No matter the reason, I always take the opportunity to ask my married female clients how they managed to get their men to commit. Marriages come in all shapes and sizes, but the one thing they have in common is that they happened. Finding out their secrets and getting paid to sell their houses is like double dipping. But like my girl Shelia always tells me, "Dip Baby. Dip."

Sheila and I grew up together in Tuskegee, Alabama where if you drove around for ten minutes, you could circle the city twice. We had two grocery stores, a handful of fast food joints, and a Main Street that only stretched about half a mile from end to end. In terms of material things, Tuskegee doesn't have much. But one famous thing we did have was Tuskegee University, the place Sheila and I attended after High School. We didn't go there when Lionel Richie or Tom Joyner did but, like them, we learned about real life from the legacy of Booker T. Washington, the Tuskegee Airmen, the faculty, and especially from those $120,000 in student loans.

That made our decision to come to Atlanta easy. See, it's only a couple of hours away, plus we could earn the kind of big city money we need to live our dreams. A few friends from college grew up there so we had a loose social network when we arrived. Still it was mostly me and Sheila. Shelia is a computer whiz who majored in Electrical Engineering and helped to build some of the credit reporting software used by Equifax after leaving her first job. But, before our big breaks, we were both living like college students. Yet Sheila is a woman after my own heart.

She began working with a startup that offered her a position before she graduated. Mostly techie-type guys from India who often spoke in their native language to keep her out of the loop. One day she went to her boss and asked for a $20,000 raise after a stellar performance evaluation. He countered that he could only give her $10,000 but that she could have it in a lump sum the following week. She nodded and walked out of his office. After cashing the check, Sheila handed in her signed resignation which contained five words: "I asked you for twenty."

My girl is cold. And she knows her worth. That's why she quit her last job paying good money when she found out the company was billing her out at triple her salary. Not that she wasn't making enough. She just felt like, since all the money came from her output, she should decide how much she gets. Today, Sheila runs her own software company and contracts herself out to write programs for ownership percentages instead of a paycheck. Needless to say, all those years we sat at Tuskegee with Dr. Scriven playing *Cashflow* really paid off.

As for me, I went into real estate straight out of college. I had a Sales & Marketing degree that taught me general concepts, but nothing about how to sell or market a specific product. All I knew was that I had no money and six months before those student loan bills kicked in. So I signed on with a small real estate firm, learned the ropes, became the highest grossing agent at the office, and opened my own company two years later.

That was four years ago. Now I'm 28 and ready for a family. But men in Atlanta are so spoiled. Even the ugly men have their pick of beautiful women because the numbers are skewed in their favor. I remember being out with Sheila one night and we watched this dude literally show his behind at a downtown bar. I turned to Sheila with my mouth hanging open and, before sipping her cosmopolitan, she raised her glass and toasted, "13 to 1".

13 to 1 is the ratio of single women to single men in Atlanta. We don't know if that is the exact ratio or if it just seems to be. Some days it feels like 13,000 to 1. When you add up all the brothers in jail, unemployed, underemployed, or undereducated, that doesn't leave very many bachelors that we would consider eligible. But that hasn't stopped us from looking.

Chapter Three

Gigi

Let's see. I'll fast forward through my college years. I was a college student and a local, so I lived in two worlds that rarely overlapped. This pretty much meant that guys on either side of the fence didn't know how to approach me. Going to college in the same small town you grew up in puts a strain on the term 'home-girl', but I didn't know anything else until I left. Most of my action happened in Atlanta, after I graduated. The first guy that approached me was Eric.

Sheila and I had saved our loan refund checks that last semester to take us through the end of the year. We shared a two-bedroom apartment inside the I-285 perimeter because the rent was dirt cheap. And dirt cheap matched our money at the time. Sheila did have a job but, back then, you had to do a week 'in the hole' before you could start working the two weeks you got paid for *next check*. If payday fell on the first Friday of your pay-week, you only got half of a check. So there we were, two weeks after we got to Atlanta, sipping sodas at *Scores Sports Bar* on Wesley Chapel on Sheila's half check.

The line outside waiting to get into this place snaked around the building like it was a nightclub. Uniformed bouncers and velvet security ropes controlled the crowd as patrons entered and exited. Yeah, it was rather 'urban' to say the least. Still, from the intelligence we'd gathered, the party was jumping in there almost every night. Normally there was a cover charge and paid re-entry fee, but when we heard about 'Free Fridays', we were the first ones to break the yellow tape. Sheila and I had both seen the advertisement about coming to *Scores* if you want to score, but we pretended to be surprised when we saw the slogan hanging on the wall. The whole place screamed while the quarterback scrambled on the big screen. But my ears were being tickled by an upbeat baritone just above our heads.

"Hey ladies can I buy you another tall one? I get free refills around here."

Maybe it had been a long week or maybe it was because his question reflected my finances, but I gave in.

"Ah, I made you laugh. If I knew that's all it took, I would've brought a two-liter."

Sheila wasn't impressed. But she seemed amused that I was. So she shot me that 'Ms. Thang" look, pinched her straw, and smiled slyly as she sipped.

"Hi. I'm Giovanni and this is my friend Sheila."

He shook our hands and introduced himself. "Eric Haynes." Eric lingered a bit with my hand then released, lightly caressing my fingertips. Sheila pinched her straw.

"Ladies, you mind if I join you?"

Sitting my drink down to prevent the glass from slipping out of my hand, I looked back and pretended to think it over. "I guess that'll be alright."

Eric checked with Sheila and she nodded agreement. When he turned to pull a chair from the next table, I could see his hard quad muscles anchoring two nicely toned cheeks and a tapered waist. He appeared to be 6 feet and slim, but well-defined and power-packed. The way he placed that chair down let me know he could lift much heavier objects with ease.

"Thanks ladies. I don't get out much, but I've been in the city for five years."

"Oh, what do you do?" We both turned toward Sheila, realizing she had spoken her first words in the conversation. I shot her a

'*Sheila?*' look, not wanting to come off as a couple of gold diggers; but I was curious, too, so I let it play out.

He cleared his throat. "Actually I'm a grad student at Clark-Atlanta, first year. Before that I was at Morehouse."

I couldn't resist. "Well, they say you can always tell a Morehouse man..." Eric saw the punch line coming and braced for the impact. Shelia and I finished in unison, "...but you can't tell him much!" We broke done wheezing. Eric sat there with his lips flattened like James Evans, Jr. on *Good Times*.

He sighed and chuckled. "No matter how many times I hear that mixed compliment, it's still *kinda* funny."

I smiled, noticing that he kept his cool while jabbing back at us to protect his dignity. "So what's your field?"

"African American Studies. I was a History major in undergrad and Clark has this joint Ph.D. program in African American and Women's Studies that is the only one in the world."

"Interesting", I said, noticing Sheila lean back in her chair and cut her eyes at me as a coded 'thumbs down' gesture.

We talked a while longer and Eric said he had to meet some friends. I gave him my business card and he promised we'd speak again soon when he stood to leave. Sheila gave him a toothless grin, waved, and slurped the rest of her Sprite.

I turned to find Sheila tucking her head, looking at me. I bit. "What?"

Chapter Four

Gigi

Sheila flattened her tongue. "You know what?"

"What? I thought he was nice. And you've gotta admit, brother was fine."

"Yeah, he looked good. But..."

"But what?"

"Girl, you know what? Don't even try it."

I stretched my eyes and titled my head. Sheila continued. "C'mon G. A Humanities major? How long do you expect to wait for him to finish school? Five, six, seven years? And what about when he finishes? Maxing out at $40,000 tops? G, be for real. We used to joke about Humanities majors in school. All those broke dudes that want to change the world...with no money. You do remember Steve, don't you?"

Steve was this guy that Sheila dated our junior year. He had locks and looked like he was chiseled from pure brass. Like Eric, Steve was also a History Major. At first it was cool. They balanced each other off well. But then everything became political between them. Steve criticized Sheila for being a technological slave of the market economy and she said he was like a Afrocentric Hippie born thirty years too late. They went at it all year long, breaking up and then having make-up sex, until she found out during finals week that Steve had slept with his study partner a few days before exams. We lost our last dead day to prepare for tests because their showdown could be heard all across campus.

"Sheila. You were hard on Steve at first."

"A woman should be hard on these dead broke men, selling dreams and expecting us to lick it up just because they say it. Besides, I *know* you're not trying to defend Steve?"

"Of course not. I'm just saying that maybe we expect too much out of guys too soon. And when they can't meet our expectations, they self-destruct."

Sheila turned her chair toward me and leaned in. "Are you saying that Steve cheating was somehow my fault?"

I quickly glanced from side to side while scooting closer. "Can you lower your voice? I don't want the whole bar to be all up in our conversation." I made a funny face and resumed. "Steve cheating was definitely not your fault. All I'm saying is that he didn't cheat because he was a History major. And if he's happy being a History major, then what's wrong with being a History major?"

Sheila pulled her head back slightly and narrowed her eyes. "Are we talking about Steve or Eric?" Sheila sat in that prissy way she always did when she thought her point was a 'gotcha'. Then she waved me off and said, "Don't answer that."

She'd caught me with my lips apart and kept talking before I could counter.

"I'll answer your last question first. Tell me how $40,000 a year matches with hundreds of thousands of dollars in student loan debt? Your new friend is probably borrowing twice as much for graduate school as he borrowed for undergrad. Besides all that, what are they actually learning? A bunch of fight-the-power jive that gets real lame when you have kids to feed and a mortgage to pay."

She did have a point, but I wasn't ready to concede.

Sheila dug in. "And to your first question, the jury is still out on whether History made Steve cheat. I mean, he kept flapping his jaws about freedom and resisting oppression. If you ask me, that's a high-dollar justification for men shirking commitment in the name of revolution. Men swear they're so slick. They ain't fooling nobody.

I can't lie and say that Steve didn't drop a lil' knowledge from time to time, but that's not productive work. If you ask me, any man that's not making something ain't up to nothing…and needs to keep walking. And on top of that, got the nerve to cheat? Girl, don't get me started."

Sheila shook her head and looked around the room. But something she said piqued my curiosity. So I gently placed my hand atop hers and asked. "Why do you think Steve cheated, for real?"

Sheila took a deep breath, then exhaled. "Because the Earth turns around the sun. Because the North wind blows north sometimes. Because the Pope is Catholic. The sky is blue. The grass is green. It was Wednesday. Girl, take your pick."

I could see the hurt well up in Sheila's eyes that she'd been masking with sarcasm since we were young. I could also tell she'd been flipping through the Nikki Giovanni anthology I kept on the coffee table. Some of the reasons she gave were quotes from the poem "Resignation"; but the lady in the poem is resigned to the fact that she loves this guy uncontrollably and no matter what.

Sheila spoke again. "G, I don't know. They never got together after we broke up and it did seem like a fling. For real, I honestly think men cheat because they can. You remember how it was at school. They could have women all around campus and we would never know it. There were so many of us and so few of them, we pretty much waited our turn until a man became available."

I leaned my face on my palm, trying unsuccessfully not to sigh.

She didn't relent. "You know I'm telling the truth, Gigi. That's why married men are so bold when they approach us."

"What do you mean?"

"I mean they know they're more like what we're looking for than most of the guys we deal with. So they figure we won't tell anybody because we're so happy to have a real man…even if it's only a piece."

I winced. This was the thoughtful side of Sheila that tapped into deep wisdom whenever she surfaced. "Sheila, you didn't…" My voice trailed off.

She lifted her chin and looked into the middle distance. "Naw, girl. I don't go out like that. I'm just saying."

I had to smile and 'Amen' the sentiment. "I feel you, Sheila. Considering the kind of men we want, pickings are slimmer here than at Tuskegee. At least we knew we were getting college educated men."

"True. But now I'm starting to think that as long as he's got hustle, I can work with him. I hate to admit it, but I think what Steve used to say about college students being slaves to the market has some truth to it."

"And?"

"And I think he's right about a lot of it. That doesn't mean I think it justifies walking around quoting Cornel West and Angela Davis all day. But college doesn't put drive in people. So if there was a guy that I found attractive, who was trying to produce something tangible, and wouldn't cheat; whether or not the brother went to college, I'd give him a shot."

I nodded slowly as a thought crossed my mind. "Okay. Then would that apply to Eric?"

"Absolutely not, G. For one thing, that's your man so you're going to have to deal with him. But secondly, he's a History major."

I shrugged. "So?"

"So I reserve the right to scratch off all History majors on general principle."

We laughed and ordered another round of high fructose corn syrup for the road.

Eric did call and we started seeing each other. Neither of us had much money or time, but we managed to eek out a couple of nights a week to share a sandwich or take walks around the Atlanta University

Center. The weekend after Thanksgiving we were walking by the Martin Luther King Chapel at Morehouse and Eric grabbed my hand.

"I need to talk to you about something."

Sheila had been quizzing me on how things were going and I'd kept my answers short and sweet to avoiding jinxing the process. I enjoyed our time together and Eric was good people. He reminded me of Steve occasionally when he started in on the social analysis, but Eric had balance. He knew how to reign it in and not let it consume our time. I felt like we really connected on many levels. "What is it?"

I knew it wasn't just me and that he felt it, too, but I'm old-fashioned so I wanted him to make the first move. Looks like my waiting paid off.

Eric swallowed. "Giovanni, you're an incredible woman and I love being with you..."

So far so good. All I had to do was keep it together and let the man get through his speech. Don't laugh. Don't cry. Just nod.

"...my mind is on you all the time and I'm finding it hard to concentrate on my studies."

What was he saying? My brain was about two seconds behind his words but I think he's saying that I'm a distraction. Is that good or bad? I'm going to keep it positive and say that it's good. Well, at least I can say that it's neutral until I get more information. Should I keep nodding? I kept nodding.

"I wouldn't be a very good Women's Studies student if I wasn't honest with you so..."

That 'so' doesn't sound like a good 'so'. I'm trying to keep the faith here, but I'm failing fast. I kept nodding.

"...so the only fair thing to do is to let you know that I'm not ready for a relationship right now; before things move too far along."

I stopped nodding. All I kept thinking was, "Those damned History majors!" It took me two weeks before I mustered up the courage to tell Sheila what had happened.

Chapter Five

Gigi

Did I mention that Sheila had a baby in college? She found out over summer break following junior year. You guessed it. Just a few weeks after catching Steve with his pants down, she started waking up feeling woozy. Since the breakup, pregnancy was the last thing on Sheila's mind but, you know how it goes. Your worst nightmare always seems to occur at the absolute worst possible time. Or so it seems in the moment.

If there could be any good news, it was that Sheila was two months pregnant in mid-May when the doctor confirmed our suspicions. She had the baby right after finals week on December 20th. We shouldn't have, but we drove to Montgomery on New Year's Eve that year and danced the night away. Sheila's mom and dad were very involved and, because they lived in town, they kept Diamond during the day while Sheila finished school. The bad news was that Steve, while not distant, wasn't helpful either. So even though he was there, he kind of faded into the background of our struggle to be happy, educated, and successful in spite of our circumstances.

Sheila also found Jesus that summer. She's not all carried away with it, but she does have her rules to live by. She prays every morning for guidance and every evening to give thanks. She goes to church on Sundays and helps out at "Hosea Feed The Hungry" on Donnelly Avenue once a month. But her absolute pet peeve and most vocal rule: no sex before marriage. Obviously, we're not together on that last one yet.

Diamond is six now, but she was barely six months when we graduated from Tuskegee. Sheila's parents volunteered to keep the baby for a year or so until she got on her feet. Good thing Diamond wasn't around during the Eric episode. After I told Sheila what went down, she seemed to hover in midair when she jumped off the couch.

"You didn't sleep with him, did you?"

I felt like I was in the principal's office. "No, we weren't that far along. We barely kissed."

Sheila sighed. "Thank you Jesus. That's a relief. But with all the secrecy, I didn't know what to think."

I understood Sheila's concern, but I didn't want to. I wanted to be in a relationship that was passionate and intimate and, well, headed somewhere. Still, I knew my wanting alone wouldn't make it happen.

I confessed. "Yeah, girl. I knew History majors weren't your favorite people so I tried to keep everything low-key until I saw some real progress."

Sheila walked to the kitchen and grabbed an apple. "So what's your take on it?"

"I honestly don't know. Things were going fine, good actually, until they just stopped. I can't really explain it. He could have saved that nerdy excuse he gave me and not wasted my time."

She took a bite and walked back over to the sofa. "You think there's someone else?"

"Girl, I don't know. I don't get that feeling, but men do lie. I guess I might feel better about that than if he dumped me because he just didn't like me."

Sheila grimaced. "G, you know my vote. Men are like wild animals. If you don't watch them 24/7, they'll pounce on anything with lipstick. Girl, I ain't playing. I'm putting surveillance cameras on my next man."

Sheila was always good at lightening my mood. "So you think it's somebody else, huh?"

She paused mid-chew and spoke with her mouth full. "Gigi, men are only in three modes: cheating, about to cheat, or just cheated. They're either going to or coming from one of those places."

My shoulders jumped up and down at that one. Even though it is rather trite, it's true that the biggest fear of women, when it comes to men, is cheating. But Sheila's expression and tone of voice turned fear into comedy for the moment.

She started talking with her hands. Whenever that happened, thoughts long pinned-up were sure to follow. "God forgive me for not telling you earlier, but men come in five basic models." Sheila held up her index finger and continued. "First you have Señor Serial Dater. He's that dude always hanging out at the club, looking for the perfect woman. And he does find her. The problem is that she only stays perfect in his eyes for two weeks or after the second date; whichever comes first. At that point he stops calling and sets off on another quest to find, yet another, perfect woman."

Sheila closed her eyes and held up two fingers this time. I threw my head back because I knew she was on a roll. "The second type is Player Player. So Player Player is that guy dating at least three women at the same time with no intention of choosing between them. His fulltime job is juggling women to keep them from finding out about each other. When one eventually figures out his game, he just replaces her on the depth chart and keeps it moving. No love lost. None ever there."

I raised my eyebrows and pressed my lips together. She'd once said she felt played by Steve. We let the silence fill the void.

I detected a residual edge in her tone as she resumed. "Next there's Larry the Lover, a.k.a. Mr. Wonderful. Yeah, Larry is a regular jewel. Larry is that guy who, like Player Player, dates multiple women who may or may not know about each other. Larry is also looking for the perfect woman like Señor Serial Dater. The problem is that Larry can't find his ideal woman because he's madly in love with parts of five different women in his life. And the perfect woman that he's pasted together in his mind doesn't actually exist. So he ends up not choosing anybody because no one compares to the imaginary lady in his head. But the funny thing about Larry is that he's probably a good dude who talks to his friends about wanting to settle down, but can't figure out why he constantly fails at love."

I chimed in. "Sheila we need to get you a talk show. You're dropping larceny like you're on CNN."

Sheila smiled with her eyes. She could always tell when I was trying to cheer her up. Hopefully it worked.

I gestured. "Okay. What else you got?"

Sheila stood up. "Then there's Tommy Time Bandit. This is the guy you never see coming. You meet. You date. You take it slow. You fall in love. You try to make plans. He's not ready. You give him some time. He's happy. You're happy. A year goes by. You become restless. You try to make plans again. He's not ready. You're angry. He's defensive. You look up at the clock. You realize you've spent good years with Tommy thinking you were working toward marriage…but that was only in *your* mind. Tommy was cool just hanging out. In his mind, he has all the time in the world to make a commitment. The problem is he figures you don't need your time, so he steals it while your biological clock is running out."

I scoffed. "You should call him Timo Time Bandit."

Sheila put both hand on her hips. "And many of these clowns are cheating and making babies with women they'll never commit to."

She waved in disgust and moved past the coffee table. I vocalized my thought. "Sheila, I'm not necessarily agreeing with you but, if you're right, what can women do about it?"

I thought better of it and rephrased. "No, what can *we* do about it?"

Chapter Six

Gigi

Even though Sheila and I grew up with both our parents, times have changed. I was just reading an AJC article that said 72% of African American children are being raised by single moms. That number now includes Sheila. Sure I know that other women are raising kids alone, too, but our situation is a state of emergency. And if what Sheila says is true, we need to figure out something quick, fast, and in a hurry.

Sheila ran to her bedroom and came back with a legal pad and pen, flipping pages. "G, I'm glad you asked. While you've been on the Love Boat with Eric, I've been praying and trying to think of a way to level the playing field."

I folded my arms. "I bet you have. What've you come up with now?"

Sheila flashed me that freeze-framed, mischievous look that Michael Jackson had at the end of the *Thriller* video. She's always scribbling inventions or conjuring up ways to improve things. I figured that's what it means to have an engineer's mind so I never made a fuss about it.

She flipped a few more pages and began her spiel. "Gigi, I've been working on a way to make it hard for men to cheat."

She scanned my expression for signs of interest, because I was usually skeptical of her schemes. But I didn't have any objections yet. "Go on."

"So I sketched out an idea for a website where women can confirm if the men that approach them are in a relationship already. That way, we can protect ourselves from some of the players that prowl the streets with a mouthful of lies."

The concept interested me intellectually so my analytical side took over. "Are you saying you want to design a webpage that tells women if a man is taken?"

"Yes."

"Okay, how does this site work? How do you get people to join? Change that. How do you get *men* to join? Sheila, I don't see men flushing their whole operation down the toilet just because this website exists."

Sheila didn't miss a beat. "True. But what if it were in their best interest to sign up?"

I straightened. "In what way?"

Sheila leaned forward. "Let's say this guy is getting closer to a young lady and he wants to be intimate. What if instead of just opening her legs like a 7-11, the woman insists that they make their relationship official in a public way?"

"You mean..."

"Yeah, I mean on this website so everybody knows this is her man and..."

I cut Sheila off this time. "...and all the other ladies know that this guy is taken."

I stared at Sheila, bobbing my head without speaking. Sheila beat me to it. "So?"

"So I like the concept. I like it a lot. But let's talk about how to make it work." I reached for Sheila's pad and flipped to a clean page. "Now, I know you can write the code, but how do you plan to make sure that people with the same name don't get mixed up? I mean, with the bank or the DMV you can use social security numbers. Shame we can't."

Sheila nodded. "You're right. Even though it *would* be tight if we could. We'd know if they have children or jobs, even what their credit scores look like. And you know those credit scores are a must."

We both guffawed and she continued. "I was thinking to use name, birth date, city, state, and email address. Pictures are optional, but would definitely be a plus to narrow things down."

"Uh-huh."

Sheila kept rolling. "It's pretty simple. Once any woman he's dating convinces him to sign up, he's in the databank. After that we can track his movements and, whenever he dates someone else that signs him up, we'll know. But more importantly, the woman he's currently seeing will know if she's dealing with Señor Serial Dater, Player Player, Larry the Lover, or Tommy Time Bandit."

I looked up from the pad, remembering an earlier question. "Hey, you said men come in five types but you only named four. What's the fifth?"

Sheila held up five fingers. "Nothing's guaranteed, but hopefully after using this site, a woman will have every reason to believe her man is Faithful Freddy with more assurance in the relationship."

I suspected that Faithful Freddy was conveniently left out...on purpose; making it clear that Sheila had doubts about his existence. But I let that go for the sake of conversation. "Sheila we have a winner here if we can solve one problem."

Sheila leaned back onto the couch. "What?"

This answer would tell me if Sheila had really thought her idea through. "What do we do about Lana the Liar?"

Sheila slanted her eyes up to the left and brought them back down. "Who's that?"

I explained. "Say I'm the lady on Fantasy Island dreaming about a guy, day and night, who doesn't even know I exist. What if I happen to come upon his personal information, like the stuff you mentioned for the login?"

Sheila nodded but remained silent. "What's to stop me from creating a fake relationship with this guy on the website and potentially ruining a future love opportunity for him?"

Sheila shrugged. "People have fake identities on Facebook all the time. So that wouldn't be unique to our site."

"True. But people aren't going on Facebook for the sole purpose of getting reliable information on a potential love interest."

Sheila agreed. I continued. "Look, this data might not be as trustworthy as death and taxes, but it has to be solid."

"Okay G, I'll work on that. But you like it?"

Sheila had a Cheshire grin awaiting my response. "With reservations…I love it. This is a big project girl. Are you sure you're up for it?"

Sheila stood and signaled for a high five. "Is Fat Albert up for another stack of pancakes?"

I high-fived her and shook my head.

Chapter Seven

Timo

My given appellation is Timotheus James Barnett. My mother loved the Bible books I & II Timothy and decided that I would wear the King James Version of their namesake. I only use the full moniker when signing legal documents or endorsing checks. I know that the slow pronunciation of my name at those times signals both unfamiliarity and disapproval from those saying it, but I'm used to it. If ever I get down about it, I think to myself that it could have always been worse. My name could have been First or Second Timothy Barnett. Mercifully, my grandmother nicknamed me Timo.

With Ricky's emergency key in hand, I unlocked the door and threw the garbage bags with my clothes inside his apartment.

When I walked in, I titled my head to the side and shook it. "Ricky man, she was tripping. I told her from the gittyup I didn't want to have kids. Now she's trying to glaze me bruh? Naw, Cuz. I ain't having it."

Ricky didn't even look up from the show he was watching. "Bruh, I told you Gigi was strictly business, didn't I? But you had to have it. Your new name is Pookie, bruh. It just keeps calling you, Timo."

Ricky laughed with the ugly face. I was unamused. "Dude, this is serious. I was in the bed, about to sleep good after a little coitus, and she starts in on the relationship quiz. Where're we headed Timo? When are we getting married Timo? It was like Final Jeopardy in that piece."

Ricky put the remote down and sighed. "Timo, y'all been kicking it for three years. For me and you, that's a good minute but, in girl time, that's like ten."

I sat in the recliner and put my feet up. Ricky continued. "So what are you going to do? Cause when a woman folds her arms and starts with the cross examination, it usually means she's tired of waiting."

I craned my neck. "Waiting on what?"

Ricky pursed his lips. "What's else? That ring."

I dropped my feet to the floor and scooted up in the chair. "I already told her..."

Ricky raised his hand. "Not to cut you off Timo, but women interpret what you say by what you do."

I knew he felt all Master Yoda right then, so I let him do his thing.

"Now while your mouth said you were just kicking it, you were beating on the bootenanny day after day...which told her emotions you were in it to win it because you stayed. So she interpreted your words as you needing time to realize what she already knew."

Ricky paused. I bit. "What's that?"

"That you were sprung and weren't going anywhere."

I waved Ricky off. "See, that's what's wrong with you brothers watching too many talk shows. Why would you listen to a woman tell a man about being a man?"

Ricky huffed. I kept at it. "Dude, I'm not Gulliver. If you think I'm going let Giovanni tie me down, you're on that stuff. Look at Sampson, bruh. Read your Bible. Staying free is biblical."

I nodded and double-pointed at Ricky as he smirked.

"Naw, she didn't tie you down." Ricky leaned to the side before continuing. "But judging from your clothes by the door, it looks like she cut you loose."

Ricky pointed back at me. I responded. "That's cold, bruh. Especially since I told her you said she was nothing but trouble."

Ricky jerked his head. "What? How're you going to front me like that?"

I closed my eyes. "Don't worry about it dude. I doubt if we'll ever see her again."

Chapter Eight

Timo

I knew I should've never moved in with Giovanni. But it seemed like the thing to do because I was over there all the time anyway and my apartment had become little more than a high-dollar storage unit. So, at the time it made sense to ditch my place and cut both our expenses. Now I'm stuck on Ricky's couch with my feet hanging off the end in pajamas and dress socks.

Ricky came out of the bathroom frowning. "Man, can you get your clothes off my floor? It'd be a shame to see Brooks Brothers suits going up in flames or in a bag waiting on the Salvation Army."

I retorted. "Whatever Rick. You're just mad because Goodwill called and asked for all their clothes back."

Ricky smacked. "Everybody's not materialistic like you, Timo. I put money into my mind, not onto my behind."

"You need to put money into some clippers and onto your tape-up."

Ricky did his Johnny Carson comeback. "Speaking of being home-less…"

I surrendered. "Alright man, you win. So what's up with you today?"

"The same thing that should be up with you: work. You do still have a job, don't you?"

"Yeah, I still have that. But the market doesn't open until nine and I don't start making calls before ten."

Ricky put on his sock. "I thought money never sleeps?"

"It doesn't. But mid-morning is the best time to make a sales pitch."

Ricky grabbed his jacket. "I wouldn't know. My clientele are up, moving around, and ready to hear my sales pitch by 8:30. See ya."

Ricky teaches middle school social studies. He's always yapping about how the Phoenicians were the first to coin money or some obscure fact about traditions in other countries. In the summers, he takes trips to places he will cover during the school year to give his students firsthand knowledge of local customs. Those kids love him. I guess that's why he's won Teacher of the Year for the past three.

And me? Well, I'm a native ATLien and was a finance major at Florida Agricultural and Mechanical University, aka FAMU, in Tallahassee, Florida. That's where I met my boy Ricky. He's from T-town and took care of me on the yard. So, when it was time to graduate, I suggested that he come to Atlanta where the salaries were high and the single women were as plentiful as in college. He came up with me for Spring Break, interviewed, and the rest is history. They don't have anything like downtown Atlanta anywhere near Tallahassee, but we go back for homecoming and to see Ricky's folks once or twice a year.

My people died when I was young, so I was raised by my Muhmaw. We used to ride the city bus down Peachtree and I would always tell her that I'd work in that big building one day. After I found out who owned it, working for Merrill Lynch was a self-fulfilling prophecy. Muhmaw passed when I was in college and Ricky's family took me in as their own.

I'm not a partner at Merrill yet, but things are looking good. My portfolio is growing and the business I bring in is making heads turn. But you can only go so far making money for somebody else. I don't want to say it's a pimp-ho relationship but…I'd be lying if I said I didn't feel like I was walking the strip with 6-inch stilettos every now and then. All is fair in love and war, and I believe that deep down to the bone. That's how I handle my business and that's how I handle my women.

Chapter Nine

Timo

Throwing Down Thursday is when me and the fellas get together to have some drinks, unwind, and see what we can see...if you know what I mean. What did I care about Giovanni? That just freed me up to laugh harder at the jokes we told about suckers under lock and key by their women. Sometimes we hit our old haunts, but tonight we decided to just kick it at this lil' soul food spot called *The Beautiful*.

Anything you could ever imagine at a black family reunion was right in front of you. Cornbread, greens, candied yams, sweet potato pie. Food so good, make your tongue lick your brain out. We pulled two small tables together and sat down with our trays. Besides me and Ricky, there was D.C., whose first name is Virgil but had been raised in Jacksonville, Florida a.k.a. Duval County. And there was Luke. Luke was actually from Indianapolis but, when he came to FAMU and discovered 2 Live Crew at an 80's party, he bought a removable gold tooth cover and started telling everybody he was from Miami. We all met in freshman orientation and have been tight ever since. D.C. and Luke came to Atlanta after the last official Freaknik and partnered on a small, residential contracting business.

D.C. wore a polo and khakis. However Luke was in full, after-five, gear: gold slip-in, wave cap, jean shorts, and a Miami Dolphins throwback jersey. As I brought my silverware to the table, the two of them were whispering.

D.C. couldn't even let me take the first bite before he started. "Say

Timo. Saw Giovanni the other day. Looking good oy, looking good. Y'all still together?"

Snickers broke out at the table. Ricky pretended to cough. Luke pounded his chest as if food had gotten stuck in his esophagus. 'Oy' was slang for boy in some parts of Florida and 'irl' was...well, you can figure it out. Normally I would have jumped on how retarded 'oy' sounds, but that would've just made me look more pathetic. I took another tactic.

"Naw, bruh. If you want her, you can have her."

By this time, Luke was wiping tears from his eyes in silent laughter. D.C. turned the knife deeper. "Timo, she hurt you like that oy? I know you're not sitting here trying to act blasé blah?" D.C. put his hand on my shoulder. "You're among friends Timo. Don't be ashamed to cry."

At that point, Ricky couldn't pretend any longer. He put his fork down and laughed in my face like Charlie Murphy. Luke and D.C. held their stomachs, preventing them from ripping open, and even I had to chuckle at the mere spectacle of it all. I waved the white flag. "Okay, okay. It does still sting a little bit. You satisfied?"

D.C. held up his hands. "I'm just saying it was cold how she did you, Timo."

I relaxed the grip on my fork. "No argument there."

Luke joined in. "Dawg, she put two hands in the middle of your back and pushed you out into the street."

I retaliated. "Who asked you, fake Mystikal?"

Finally the ridicule of the table eased off of me for a second. Ricky stepped in and acted as peacemaker. "Timo, I already told the boys what went down. It's us, bruh. Tell us how you feel."

The table sat still, no blinks. I nodded and gave it to them straight. "Aite. I feel like she straight played me."

I took a sip of my beverage and continued. "Man, I was with that girl for three years. Never cheated, never lied. Not even once. And you know how I used to do."

D.C. agreed in a muffled tone. "You ain't lying."

Luke started to guffaw, then elbowed D.C. when I looked over.

I continued. "It's not like I couldn't have. I had plenty of women buying me drinks. I spit a little game, but never took any numbers or anybody up on offers."

Luke chimed in. "But you did take the drinks."

I shrugged. "Hey, a brother was thirsty."

"Awww whatever!" The crew broke out into raucous laughter, waving their hands to dismiss my excuse.

Ricky took command of the noise. "See Timo, you got this thing all wrong."

D.C. turned his chair. "Oh yeah? Do tell Ricky Lake."

Ricky's last name is Lane, but when D.C. found him watching talk shows in the Student Union freshman year, he's been 'Ricky Lake' ever since.

Ricky let it slide and kept looking at me. "You think she did you wrong, right?"

I sat up straight. "Absolutely."

"And you did nothing to her?"

"Like what?"

Luke and D.C. scooted their plates forward and put their elbows on the table.

Ricky bent his lips. "Like leading Giovanni on? Like letting her think you were seriously considering marrying her? Need I say more?"

D.C. tapped Luke on the forearm. "That sounds pretty wrong to me. Does that sound wrong to you?" Luke nodded. D.C. turned. "What about you, Timo?"

I placed my hands onto my chest. "I didn't do her wrong. I told her from Jumpstreet that I was not looking to get married. I was honest with her 100%. The problem is women can't take honesty. They want you to lie to them, because the truth hurts."

Ricky sighed. "The truth does hurt. And it's hurting you bad right now."

Luke and D.C. were back at it so I decided to set the record straight. "I know you're not talking, Ricky? As I recall, you were the master at bow-wow-wow yippee-yo-yippe-yay! So, don't get too holy on me up in here."

Luke lifted his knuckles for a fist bump. "Rick you were dirtier than 2 Live back in the day."

Ricky stared at Luke with no expression, leaving him hanging in the air. "And so was yo mama, bruh."

Wheezing, D.C. grabbed Luke's wrist. "Put your hand down, oy."

Chapter Ten

Timo

My condo search has been crazy over the last few months. I hate to admit it, but I haven't found anything as cozy as Giovanni's place. Everything I've seen feels so cold and sterile. So I decided to put that on hold and ask Ricky if we could room together again like we did in college. I'd have a place to stay and he'll have someone paying half his bills. It's a great deal if you ask me.

Ricky seemed a little hesitant at first. But after I called his mom, he was forced to take me in. He's always talking about me learning my lesson. The only lesson I've learned so far is that it's easier to be single in the daytime. At night, it's Hell. *No Woman No Cry* only makes sense when the sun is shining. Guess that explains why lone wolves howl at the moon.

To take my mind off things, I plan to totally immerse myself into work. I'm scouting some big clients this year and saving my money to make a move on my own. Meanwhile patience is my virtue. That and the grind. When I wake up, my alarm is bumping Rick Ross' *Hustlin'* and I have sticky notes posted on the bathroom mirror that remind me of my goals. Ricky says if I forget to bring home toilet paper today he's gonna use a handful of my reminders as wipes. I figure I'd better write that one on my hand.

Chapter Eleven

Gigi

Sheila and I talked off and on about the site for another six months before I finally convinced her that you couldn't stop men from cheating; well not directly anyway. But a worldwide website that educated women on the five different types of men and how to find Faithful Freddy would be the next best thing. So we kept the same basic design, but changed the emphasis to helping women find a man who will commit. Sheila told me as long as the site makes it harder for at least one brother to cheat, count her in.

Keeping the data reliable was no longer a problem either. All people had to do was enter their name and email address to join and they could read articles, send in anonymous letters, and read posted responses like an advice column. In no time the database would grow and grow. But the site had to be built first. That was Sheila's department, so I gave her some space while she got the prototype done. Still, the concept lacked something that I couldn't quite put my finger on.

Meanwhile, things were picking up with my listings and Sheila had just begun the Equifax project. During that period, our incomes reached six figures and we both bought our own places. Sheila sent for Diamond and got her enrolled in pre-K while I started dating Timo. I know I promised to tell you about the next time I saw him, but there are a few more things you should know first.

One thing is that I learned a trick or two from those old birds at my first real estate agency. The biggest is that most of selling homes is building rapport so people feel it's a status symbol to buy from *you*.

You don't do that by plastering your face all over some tawdry billboard next to Jimmy's Heating and Air. Instead, you attend soirées and establish a reputation for selling homes to those with discriminating palates. All that means is you've got to make people with lots of money feel that it's in their best interest to call you when they want to buy or sell.

Those women at my first agency got rich selling the same houses, over and over, to different people. At first I fought it. But I finally accepted that selling upper-crust homes is about selling yourself as part of the house. You have to be up on every detail including the builders, the previous owners, and especially the current occupants. If you're not, people with money will eventually buy the house; just not from you. But if you're the listing agent, no matter how much they try to wriggle off that hook, they always have to come see mama if they want what belongs to mama. Still, as the listing agent, knowing your stuff can mean the difference between half the commission or all the commission. And for most working folks, that other half might be half a year's salary.

I stepped out my car at Whole Foods and spotted a familiar face floating toward me. "Mildred! Hey girl. How've you been?"

The top selling realtor at my former agency before I got there, Mildred owed me a favor. I'd cut her in on a referral commission worth $5,000 a while back. That's the kind of card you don't play right away. Not a Big Joker. You just let it rest in your hand until you need it.

"Hello Giovanni. How are you, Dear?"

"Girl, I'm fine. Just trying to get some free range chicken. You?"

Mildred was early 60's, rocking St. John suits and Armani pumps, and slim. She tried to play that untouchable sophisticate role, but it was common knowledge that Mildred was a country girl who loved horses. That is, she loved to play them, anytime she could. To do that and live large took money, and lots of it. So, despite the occasional flushing of her cheeks when we exchanged pleasantries, to cross me was to jeopardize a future date with the ponies.

Mildred showed all of her teeth. "I am well. I see you are also doing well for yourself."

Mildred eyeballed my Benz like it was the only man at a bachelorette party. It was nice. Big body S-6, peanut butter leather seats, and the personalized tag that read: "GGSELLS".

I retorted. "It's just something that gets me from A to B."

We did the 'you're so fake' laugh. Mildred resumed. "Well, I've been invited to the Christmas party of the year. Sure wish you could come but invitations were limited."

Her shark smile returned. *It's like that, huh?* I thought to myself and smirked.

And so I began. "Where's the party?"

"The Grant Park District. Lots of old money."

Mildred placed her hand on my shoulder and knitted her brow; sympathetically patting while rendering her best Diahann Carroll imitation. "Be patient, Giovanni. You'll soon have entrée into those circles but, my Dear, dues must be paid."

"I couldn't agree more Mildred." She bobbed her head with the slow nod of understanding and consensus.

I reached for my Joker. "Do you remember that favor you owe me?"

Mildred's jaw dropped slack. I left the parking lot without free-range chicken. Instead I had an invitation to the swankiest shindig of the season and a rearview look at a woman impeccably dressed, but whose flawless face had cracked into a million pieces.

Chapter Twelve

Gigi

Sheila was thrilled to get out of the house. Since we'd moved up a bit, we had issues adjusting to our new class status. The usual bars and clubs didn't do it for us anymore. Still, we enjoyed a stroll through Atlantic Station every once in a while.

Tonight was different. The invitation allowed for two, so Sheila got a sitter and we were on our way.

I merged into traffic and asked, "Girl, is Diamond going to be okay?"

"Yeah. Ms C. is good people. She takes care of Diamond like that's her own daughter. I'll be lucky if Diamond wants to come back home tonight."

"Sounds like you're in good hands."

"We are, G. And we've bonded so well in the past year, it's like we were never apart."

"I heard that."

Sheila peeked at the address on the invitation. "I see membership does have its privileges."

"Naw, girl. You just have to play a lil' spades when life puts a deck of cards in your face."

Sheila shook her head. "You're really wild. You know that lady is at home telling Jesus on you."

I wagged my finger. "No see, you're wrong. Jesus is the one who gave us this invitation on my birthday weekend. Mildred just opened her mouth and talked her way out of my blessing."

Sheila pointed at me. "Well you tell Ms. Mildred I said, 'Let Him use you honey. Let Him use you!" We screamed breathlessly down Peachtree Industrial.

When we pulled up, Sheila hesitated before opening her door.

"G, there're no vampires in there, right? I'm just saying. The party spot looks like it could easily double as a haunted house."

Sheila did have a point. But everybody who's anybody in this business understands that the real money is in historic homes. That's why I dug my heels in and parlayed that invitation right out of Mildred's atrophied hands.

"Sheila, this is a Queen Anne style, Victorian mansion and Captain James A. Burns began building it in 1864 after the Battle of Atlanta. He was a Union soldier during the Civil War and decided to settle here when the fighting was done. The home was completed in 1868 and those castle looking things are called turrets."

Sheila squinted and scrunched her nose. "Girl, how do you know all that?"

I air-buffed my nails. "You know how I do. To sell homes at this level, you've got to pretty much know who built it, who has ever lived in it, and why anybody moved out of it. Girl I did so much internet research, I should have a Master's Degree in the history of this place."

"I know that's right. But G, it's more than the money for you. You've been looking at these old houses ever since we were kids. I used to see you staring at those big abandoned houses in Tuskegee. That one near the funeral home especially; and the other one by the old VA Hospital. Girl, if I didn't come get you, you probably would've stared at those old houses from dawn to dusk."

I dropped my eyes to my lap, took a deep breath, and looked up again. "You're right Sheila. I've always been mesmerized by 19th century homes. They're simple and complex at the same time. Parties and pain, black and white people all mixed up into a beautiful building that will tell it all if you just pay attention."

After I finished, Sheila let me enjoy the gravity of my moment before she spoke. "Yeah, I know your favorite was 'The Oaks'. After becoming a tour guide for that place, I knew your love affair with old houses would last forever. Matter of fact, this house kind of favors that one a little."

I turned and bent my knee in the seat, eyes wide and mouth agape. 'The Oaks' is the historic home of Booker T. Washington built by Tuskegee students in 1900 and is a red brick, Queen Anne style home as well. It's now maintained by the National Parks Service.

Sheila had done it again. "Girl, you know too much about me."

She nudged my leg. "Well G, we're both living our dreams. My thing is computer code and yours is old houses. I get that."

"Then you get me. And that's why you're my girl for real, for real."

We laughed and hugged.

After settling back into our seats, Sheila frowned and pointed. "Are those tombstones in the front yard?"

I followed her hand and nodded. "Yes ma'am. Captain Burns and two of his soldier buddies."

"But G, this is Grant Street."

"Yeah girl, I know. Still, folks with money have been doing whatever they want longer than Grant Street has been here." I shrugged and continued. "C'mon Sheila, let's go inside."

She resigned. "Alright. But it looks like we should be here for Halloween instead of Christmas."

I harrumphed. "Girl you *stay* crazy."

We both started up the sidewalk as my car alarm chirped.

Sheila remarked. "I guess you never can be too careful, huh? Especially with rich people around."

Sheila was right. Most people stole cars for thrills, not need. And the rich are certainly not immune to thrill seeking. So, just to be safe, I made my alarm chirp again so I'd be sure to find my car just the way I'd left it.

Chapter Thirteen

Gigi

We approached the house and I spied granite steps that mirrored the granite of the foundation. But before I could comment, my attention immediately shifted to the craftsmanship and detail of the wrap-around front porch. The original porch had been badly weathered in the photos online, but the new owners restored it to a state that may have exceeded its former glory.

If you poll black people on the Confederacy, you'll usually get a unanimous thumbs down. But if you poll those same folks on front porches, you'll get more thumbs up than Siskel and Ebert. Front porches are premier socializing stations; fully equipped for gossiping, people watching, lemonade drinking, and goodnight kissing. The uses of a solid front porch are endless. And a huge, beautiful wrap-around porch? Child, please. Heaven on Earth.

I allowed my hand to linger on the rail and wondered about the things it had seen. Sheila gave me the mafia head nod, so I left my questions unanswered; hopeful that the interior could provide more clues.

Crossing the threshold, the decor sparkled just as the article had described. An archived spread in the Atlanta Journal & Constitution presented the home in much of its splendor. But like Solomon said when he actually saw the Queen of Sheba: 'Half the story had never been told.' I simply had to spend some time alone with this house.

"Sheila, I'll meet you in ten minutes at the punchbowl. I want to take a good look at this place."

Sheila waved her hand. "Go ahead and work your magic. I'll check on those hors d'oeuvres and make my way down to the figgy pudding."

I nodded and headed straight for the formal parlor.

Ecstasy was the first word that popped into my mind. The fragrance of aged mahogany sank deep into my nostrils and framed the elegant furnishings of the room. The creamy fabric blended seamlessly with muted persimmon accents, creating a classic, yet lived-in, feel. Bradbury and Bradbury coverings ushered me to a period when walls and ceilings were not merely painted, but designed. The presentation was literally a feast for my eyes and I couldn't move, stuffing my senses.

"You like the nativity scene?" A dancing voice slowly brought me back to consciousness.

Before I could catch myself, I spoke. "Huh?"

The voice tittered and its owner placed a hand on my shoulder. "The nativity scene?"

I recovered enough to glance sideways and focus before responding. "I do. A life-sized Fontanini nativity scene is perfect in an exquisite setting like this."

"Hmmm. I'm impressed. You know your Fontanini."

I turned to face my complimenter. "Thank you."

She had a tray of apple martinis in her hand. Fiftyish. Wavy black hair with wide brown eyes. High, fleshy cheekbones—but not too fleshy. Stylish black evening dress that had a velvety appearance with a satin sheen.

She extended a greeting. "I'm Storie, ma'am. Would you care for a drink?"

I reciprocated. "Giovanni George. Nice to meet you Storie."

I found her name fascinating for its beauty and simplicity. I mused about how my family would have mutilated it into 'Store' or 'Ri Ri'. But I liked Storie. I wondered what tales she had to tell.

"Nice to meet you Ms. Giovanni. Lovely name."

I smiled at her Southern charm and dove right in. "Thank you, Storie. So what can you tell me about this house and the people who live here?"

Storie tilted her head to the side in thought. "Well, I can tell you a lot about the house. In fact I can give you a tour after I serve this tray of drinks. But the people who live here are an eccentric bunch. That would take more time."

"I've got all the time in the world. Like some of the people in this crowd, I'm a real estate agent and I'd love to list this house when the owners are ready to sell it." Instinctively I handed her my card.

Storie looked it over and tossed it onto the tray. "Georgian Reality. Your company?"

I beamed a relaxed smile. Most people didn't catch the play on my name in the title. They usually think 'Georgian' reflects the state. But, for me, it showcases the intention of Giovanni George to take over the Georgia real estate market...on the high end.

I nodded.

"Very impressive." Storie held up a finger. "Don't go far. I'll be back directly."

She moved away, delivering beverages to appreciative attendees, and I sauntered through the olive and rose-toned den over to the dining room. Sheer delight. The ivory-colored paneling set the stage for the alabaster chandelier hanging over the 300 year old, cherry wood table. The article had depicted this room exactly. Standing there made the words levitate from the page.

I'd just thought about Sheila when I felt a nudge. "Are you ready?"

Chapter Fourteen

Gigi

A trayless Storie stood to my left this time, again pleasantly amused.

I smiled at myself. "I am."

Storie linked my arm and led me back toward the living room. She leaned in and whispered. "Before we begin, I'd like to introduce you to someone."

I went along for the ride, curious; more to know what Sheila had gotten into than who I was about to meet. Those priorities changed places quickly.

Near the landing of the grand, teak wood staircase, stood a tall, mocha colored man. Late fifties, at least 6'2", impeccably dressed, sporting a flawlessly manicured, Magnum P.I. mustache. Can you say 'chocolata'?

Storie brought me close and hugged my arm as she spoke. "Walters, I'd like you to meet Ms. Giovanni George. She is an independent realtor and has a fine eye for décor."

The refined sculpture extended his hand. "Walters Killingsworth. Pleased to make your acquaintance."

Beyond his right shoulder, I could see Sheila mouthing "Who is that?" with a wild expression, insistently wiggling both index fingers.

I remembered myself. "Uh…nice to meet you, too."

Maybe I put a little too much emphasis on the 'you' for proper business etiquette. But I was having a hard time concentrating on that. This man was beyond attractive. He was stately.

Walters gave a shallow bow with both hands clasped in a Tibetan fashion around his drink. "Giovanni, welcome to our home."

Was my mouth hanging open? Or maybe a piece of my face fell onto the floor. But I thought I just heard this beautiful black man say that this palatial Victorian mansion was his. "You live here?"

Walters raised his fluted glass to me with a good-natured chuckle. "We both do. Didn't Storie tell you?"

You could have bought me for a penny. Here I thought this sister was the maid because she was serving drinks, and she turns out to be the owner of the house. I looked at Storie with a mixture of apology and egg on my face.

Storie gave him a coy smile. "Walters, Giovanni and I have just met and I am about to begin a proper tour. See you in a few moments, Love."

Storie turned to me. "Let's have a look around, shall we?"

I nodded, mute. I shot Sheila the 'be-back-in-five' signal and synchronized steps with Storie.

Approaching the dining room, I went into confession mode. "You have a lovely home. No. It's beyond lovely; it's regal."

"Thank you Giovanni. I apologize for not mentioning it earlier. I sometimes like to see what people think of the house without knowing who I am. It helps me to understand with whom I'm keeping company."

I hazarded the question. "So, did I pass?"

Storie stopped and put her hand on her hip. "If you didn't, I would never have introduced you to my man."

Spoken like only a black woman could.

We traded knowing glances and became fast friends. I got the abbreviated tour that day, but Storie invited me back many times that next year. Each time she shared a bit more history about the house and showed me features that I hadn't noticed the time before. I learned that she and Walters were both realtors who dealt in higher end homes and that both their offices were located on the premises. I guess there's no better way to sell your ability to list a home than showing the client that your crib rivals or surpasses their own.

That's why, about two months ago, I was confused when Storie called to tell me they were selling the house.

Chapter Fifteen

Gigi

I rearranged my schedule to meet Storie at the house and phoned Sheila to tell her why I couldn't make our lunch appointment.

"G, are we still on for tonight?"

"You know it Sheila. I've got a feeling that we're close. If it works, this site could literally change the world."

"I hear you, G. But what would change the world is if brothers acted like men and stepped to us with honesty and respect."

"You're absolutely correct. But I think we have to help our brothers do right."

"I agree. So make sure you're here on time, G. I told Diamond you'd be here for six, and you know she'll be looking out the window at 5:45."

"I know, girl. I promise I'll be there before time. Need me to bring anything?"

Sheila snorted. "Do you ever?"

"I'm just asking."

With that we said our goodbyes and I maneuvered into the Grant Park District.

After several turns, I braked in front of Captain Burns' grave and high-tailed it up the steps to the doorbell. I'd arrived early so I waited in Storie's office while she finished a business call. I couldn't help but notice an embroidered rug that hung on the right wall, close to her desk. It displayed a set of Victorian suitors dueling on horseback and, in the background, a lady stood off to the side attended by her handmaiden.

Even though the office is on the first floor, the half-moon window flooded the scene on the rug with sunrays. Usually I would have admired the painstaking trim detail of the window, but I guess you admire things most that you've seen least. In my case, it was men fighting for the chance to court a woman. That was more than rare in my world.

After Storie finished her call, we moved into the kitchen area to brew some tea. I loved the kitchen because it contrasted the classic theme of the house with a modern sensibility. The granite countertops, cherry cabinets, and professional-grade appliances played well against the Greek key design in the tile work. Nevertheless, we eventually settled onto a glass-covered area with a bricked base where I could see straight down about fifty feet underground.

I asked Storie about it to break the ice.

She took a sip of her English Chamomile and reclined. "That well used to sit on a porch before we extended the kitchen. As children, we fetched water there. It was sentimental for us so we intentionally incorporated it into the remodeling plan. The well is 55 feet deep and we installed lighting on the glass top so Walters and I could always see our childhood memories anytime we wished."

I must have grimaced because Storie's eyes flickered on beat with my befuddled look.

She set her teacup on the saucer and clasped her hands. "I know you came to find out why we are moving, so I think I should start from the beginning."

I was all ears; silent but urging her to continue.

"Walters and I grew up in the Grant Park area, yet under different circumstances. Walters lived nearby with his mother and I lived inside the mansion with mine. Both women were domestics for a family that owned the property long after Captain Burns died. Walters and I saw each other everyday, played together, and became childhood sweethearts. His mother eventually scraped up enough money to buy a small home on the far end of the street; close enough that he could see the mansion in the distance from his steps."

The nostalgia in her voice told me she could vividly see the thoughts she spoke. I stretched my eyes to dry the moisture.

"While our mothers cleaned and waited on the owners, Walters and I did odd jobs like fetch water from this well or dump ashes from the fireplaces into the underground tunnels."

I had to ask. "How much time did you two spend in those tunnels?"

Storie blushed. "I don't recall exactly. But I can tell you that we always volunteered to help each other dispose of the ashes; even the least amount."

I craned my neck. "You know I'm over here taking notes, right?"

Storie patted her grin with a napkin and continued. "One September day, the owners announced that they would be selling the house and that the new owners had their own staff. I was sixteen at the time. Mother and I moved back to Roanoke with family and Walters stayed here in Atlanta with his mother. Needless to say I was heartbroken. To lose the only home I had ever known and the love of my life in the same week devastated me."

Involuntarily, I clutched for pearls I wasn't wearing.

Storie remained in thought. "Still, Mother had saved since I was a child for me to attend University. When I received a partial scholarship to Howard, it was settled that I would matriculate there. I studied English as an undergraduate, maintaining a healthy fascination with Black Victorian society. Since I grew up within a Victorian structure, I found my interest only natural."

She stopped, not to drink her tea, but to smile with her eyes closed. I held my breath for what was coming next.

"Exactly one year to the day in September that I'd left Atlanta, I exited my morning Composition class and who stood propped against a wall dressed in the most dashing autumn suit I'd ever seen?"

I said the name in a questioning swoon. "Walters?"

Storie bit her bottom lip and nodded rapidly. I melted.

"I stopped in my tracks, frozen. My heart thundered. I was convinced he saw my blouse fluttering. Even in the crisp breeze of fall, there was not enough air to fill my lungs."

I couldn't take it. I rested my forehead on the glass top and looked deeply into the well before rising. "So what did you say?"

Storie shook her head. "Nothing. Nothing at all."

She paused, widened her eyes, and continued. "As I stood there, speechless, he gave me a tender smile and said, 'You think you can get rid of me that easily?' Since then, we have never been apart."

I could have died right there from an aching heart. Storie sensed how moved I was and sat a cube of tissue beside my hand.

"Walters enrolled in Howard that day and worked his way through school as an architect's apprentice. Back then, architects not only designed buildings but they also knew how to physically build them. So Walters studied Business Administration in school while learning real estate design and construction on his job. We were married after my eighteenth birthday, finished school together, and raised two beautiful children who are now grown and doing well."

I could see that Storie was genuinely pleased with how her life had turned out.

"It was not without struggle. Sometimes there was much more thin than thick. But we worked together and combined our gifts to build a successful nest egg in the Maryland real estate market; and really had no intentions of leaving the area."

My mother always told me my favorite game was 'connect the dots'. Maybe I was OCD, but I had a high-intensity need to know how Storie and Walters ended up here. "So what brought you back?"

"Well, by that time both of our mothers were deceased. But

Walters had promised his mother, before he left Atlanta to find me, that one day he would buy this house. When the property came up for sale, he took me on a surprise trip to Atlanta and arranged for us to have a private showing. We walked in places we were never allowed to as children. And we visited places we knew all too well. We began to reminisce and envision improving the house and, the next thing you know, we were at the closing table."

I was on both elbows by this time, with chin in hand and fingertips touching my cheeks.

"I insisted on sealing this well myself when we expanded the kitchen. I had pulled enough buckets of water from here to last a lifetime. No one else should have to."

I looked at the magnificent job they had done in the kitchen, admiring and wondering what else Storie wanted to seal off. "And the butler's pantry, beneath the servants' stairway?"

Storie shook her head. "That didn't exist when Mother and I lived here. I watched her work twice as hard because the home was not designed with consideration for those who kept it running. So the next year, we constructed the butler's pantry with a built-in hutch and surrounded it with Venetian marble in honor of our parents. My mother and I slept in the servant's quarters on the third floor; which suffered heavily from termite damage. This past year we tore that room down to the bones and restored it to the condition in which it should have been maintained."

At that statement, I squinted. "Storie, I thought I would understand more, but I actually understand less. And it makes your phone call today even more odd."

Storie sipped her cooling tea in expectation of my question.

I asked. "So why in the world would you want to leave a place that you put so much work into making perfect?"

Storie lifted her palms, cradling the air around my face. "You've got it. That's exactly why we must leave. Our work here is done..."

I lingered as Storie's reasoning dawned on me. But nothing could have prepared me for what came next.

Firmly staring into my eyes with thumbs on the rim of her tea cup, she finished her statement. "...which is also why we want you to represent us as our real estate agent."

Chapter Sixteen

Gigi

Somebody must have caught me because I know I fainted. I thought I was too young to wear a medic alert bracelet, but when another real estate agent offers you a commission worth $200,000 on their own residence, you too might fall where you can't get up. Somehow I made it to Sheila's house, without smelling salt, but told her enough on the phone that she was standing in the street when I pulled up.

Sheila opened my car door. "G, I need you to start from the beginning and tell me everything you remember."

I walked into Sheila's well-appointed condo greeted by a diving hug that sent me stumbling onto the sofa, giggling.

Diamond and I played the tickle game and it did me some good to release a lot of that nervous energy.

After some 'girl-let's-catch-up talk', Diamond forgot about me and rediscovered Disney Channel's ability to enchant all ages.

Sheila weighed in. "So Gigi, what did you say?"

"Honestly Sheila, my tongue was so heavy it was hard to swallow. She told me to go home and come back in a week. They would already be gone but they'd have the keys, contract, and disclosures sent to my office."

Sheila stretched her lips. "Sounds like sister-girl means business."

I nodded. "I know that commission means business. Big business. Girl, that would pay off all my student loans and set me straight."

"I *know* that's right. But G, why do you think they would give away that much money if they could keep it for themselves?"

"I asked her that on the way out. She said it's difficult to sell your own house; especially when you live in it."

Sheila concurred. "She does have a point. You've always said that yourself about people who insist on selling their home themselves."

"Yeah, you're right. But most of those 'For Sale By Owners' are just being cheap. They eventually end up coming to realtors anyway. But this is different. These folks are in the business. They know more than enough to sell their house. As nice as that house is, they wouldn't even have the usual problem with white people not wanting to buy from black people. In fact, I feel confident that less than a week after it goes on the market, there'll be a bidding war and they'll get much more than the asking price."

Sheila grinned. "And that's good, right?"

"It's a dream come true. But that's just it. It's too good to be true. And that's what bothers me."

Sheila smirked. "Humph. Well it doesn't bother me. You heard what Rev said Sunday, didn't you?"

I waited for the revelation.

The Holy Ghost spoke through Sheila. "Receive it!"

I jumped to my feet and snapped three times from side to side. "Oh, I'm going to receive it. You can believe that."

Following our female end zone celebration, I nestled back into the lounge chair and covered myself in the knitted throw. "Thing is, even though the commission give-away is confusing, I understand it on another level."

Sheila recoiled on the loveseat. "How so?"

"Sheila, you didn't hear the way she told me that story today. I almost feel like they don't care about the money because they have each other."

We sat in tangible silence.

"Still, the last thing she said is playing over and over in my head."

"What?"

"Storie said that when I get the keys and do the walk through, if I look deeply enough, I'll find what I need."

"Well, let me know when you go so I can find what I need, too."

I couldn't resist. "Sheila, I don't think they left any Mandingo computer wizards tied up in the basement."

Sheila rejoined. "Oh, you got jokes, huh? Well, Ms. Thang, what are *you* looking for if I might ask?"

I paused a second too long.

Sheila pounced. "I see I struck a nerve. G, you've been looking for Prince Charming your whole life and you know it."

I pretended to ignore Sheila. She didn't let up. "Who knows? Maybe you'll find him in the bottom of that well."

Feigning offense, I turned away unable to shake Storie's words about looking deeply enough. *I do have my likes and dislikes*, I mused. I like the cool sensation of satin fabric draped lightly against my body. I dislike carpet that is too stiff to be felt between my toes. I like the first crisp morning of autumn because I can anticipate bright yellow and red hues on the trees. And I dislike, above all else, the feeling that men have an advantage over us in relationships.

I turned back to Sheila. "Maybe I'm naive. I'll accept that possibility. Still, that doesn't get them off the hook."

Sheila drew her head and neck back, scrutinizing me. I kept going. "Close your mouth, you know it's the truth."

Sheila responded. "What's the truth?"

"That men have the upper hand in the courting ritual. Good or bad. Right or wrong. They all stick together. That's the biggest thing men have going for them. They are loyal to their system."

Sheila cocked her head to the side. "What's gotten into you all of a sudden? Usually I'm the one dumping on our brethren. You're stealing my lines."

"I know. But your question got me thinking about what I really want. And this goes to the heart of what I think is missing in the website concept: I want Faithful Freddy. And I want him to be beautiful. And I know he exists for sure since Storie told me about her life."

Sheila folded her hands. "So what was her secret?"

"That's the thing. In all the excitement, I forgot to ask. Normally, I wouldn't be slipping like that."

Sheila put her arm around me and agreed. "Yeah, that is uncharacteristic of you and we will definitely cross that bridge when we get to it. But right now, we're going to celebrate that two hundred thousand with some Grand Marnier."

Chapter Seventeen

Gigi

One week later, Sheila and I were headed over to Grant Park to do the realtor walk-through with keys in hand. Houses show differently empty than when furnished. Buyers get to see every scratch and groove in the floor or hole in the wall when the property is empty. Furnishings hide those blemishes and sometimes create a false impression of what life will be like when the new owners arrive. However, in homes of this caliber, it is common for the buyer to make an offer that includes the dwelling as well as the furniture. Naturally the Killingsworths left everything as is.

Storie and Walters have a summer home in Virginia Beach and transitioned there the day after our conversation. That made my job easier. No need to schedule when the house could be shown. In that slot I can type 'Show Anytime'; assuming a pre-qualified buyer makes the request.

The aroma of the woodwork hit our noses as I turned the key. Sheila double-timed it over to a window.

"G, let's get some air circulating so we can take a good look around. Treat me like my money is longer than twenty inch Malaysian weave down my back."

I stood in the middle of the living room, closed my eyes, and inhaled a nose full of good vibrations. The Killingsworths have great energy and that certainly helps when buyers are on the premises. Early in my career I listed a home that had been the scene of a murder. Even though the property was gorgeous with incredible landscaping, the first three potential buyers refused to finish the walk through because the home didn't feel right. None of them knew about the murder but, my guess is, they sensed it in a way beyond conscious knowledge.

I smiled broadly in response to Sheila. "I'll show you every nook and cranny there is to see."

So off we went. Sheila and I were determined to explore each one of those five bedrooms, three and one-half baths, ten fireplaces, seven porches, and sixty-three windows; seven of which are pocket windows stretching from floor to ceiling. I intended to count them all so that my knowledge of the home would be unshakeable. We started up the wooden staircase with handcrafted balusters supporting the reconstructed railing.

Sheila remarked at the base. "Gigi, why do some parts of the railing look different?

Sheila had a keen eye for detail, even in passing. She also expected me to know everything about every house we were in together. I couldn't let her down.

"Believe it or not, after the Captain and his family died, the house was converted into a brothel during the Great Depression."

Sheila lightly caressed the rail. "You mean these blue-bloods allowed hookers to set up a red light district in Grant Park?"

I shrugged. "Well, I guess so."

"G, it just goes to show you. If men will pay to be with a woman, even when food is scarce, who really has the power? We just haven't figured out how to use it."

I concurred and added another factoid. "After that, the home became a boarding house. That's what happened to the rail."

"What?"

"With all the people living here in desperate times, pieces of such an ornate railing were stolen and the Killingsworths did the best they could to restore it after acquiring the property. Given the period, a carpenter today can only approximate the craftsmanship."

Halfway up Sheila joked. "Gosh G, I feel like I'm climbing Mt. Everest to meet the Dalai Lama. Don't they have an elevator?"

I kept walking without looking back. "No ma'am. This is your cardio workout for today."

Sheila snickered. "Just know that when I hit the last step, I'm finding a place to get horizontal for a minute."

We reached the third floor and came upon the old servants' quarters that now served as a guest room. This was the area where Storie spent her childhood nights with her mother, dreaming of love, better days, and far away places. It wasn't cramped like I imagined it would be. Instead, the room took on a spaciousness because of the sage tones, crisp linens, translucent draping, and sitting area that must have provided Storie with a sacred place to read and watch the seasonal leaves fall and bloom again.

Sheila commented. "Gigi, this is like a baby doll's room. It's so neat I almost don't want to lie in this bed."

I caught Sheila just before she plopped and guided her to the cushion in the window seat. We chatted a few minutes before inspecting the rest of the floor and heading down to the main.

The master bedroom stood off the back of the house in an area used by previous owners for storage.

Sheila crossed her arms. "Storie must've let him decorate this one."

The room did have a masculine quality to it. Dark browns and earth tones coupled with oval portraits and pedestal lamps gave the feel of a rustic cabin in the woods or a sea vessel.

I responded. "Storie told me Walters believes Captain Burns slept in this bedroom. Now don't repeat this until I make the sale, but both he and his wife died in the home and..."

I paused. Sheila urged. "And?"

I grinned. "Maybe I shouldn't tell you."

Sheila tugged at my sleeve. "G, don't play. Tell me."

I straightened my blouse and cleared my throat. "Alright already. Geesh."

I took my time brushing my shoulders before continuing. "If you must know, Walters swears to ghost sightings back here and in the lower portions of the house."

Sheila shook her head. "I knew it. I knew it. I hate to say I told you so..."

"No you don't."

Sheila stopped shaking her head. "You're right, I don't. But I told you so. The moment I laid eyes on this place I knew something was wrong. And with those giant tombstones in the yard, I almost expect ghosts to float around here re-enacting the Civil War."

This time it was me shaking my head at Sheila.

She followed-up. "Besides, Captain and Mrs. Burns are probably chapped on the hind parts that black people own the house instead of simply working in it."

I shot her the 'bulls-eye' nod and wink. "Uh-huh. I'm sure Cappie and the Mrs. are sore about the whole role reversal thing, but check this out."

I lowered my voice. "Walters says the ghosts are black folks."

Sheila responded from the corner of her mouth. "You don't say?"

She looked over both her shoulders, then back to me. "And how long has this been going on?"

"Storie says since they were teenagers. Just before she moved to Virginia, she and Walters ventured into the tunnels to dump ashes and say their goodbyes. According to her, it was their special place. Well, while they were dumping their buckets, Storie says they saw the silhouette of a woman with a book in her hand, extending it toward them. Girl, she said they were so scared, they ran out of there like banshees and never went back."

Sheila shook her feet as if she had on track spikes. "G, that sounds like a good idea to me."

"Me, too…after I finish this inspection."

Sheila nodded. "Girl, you're right. I'm tripping. I'm staying, too. Because for 200 G's, a ghost can fart in my dinner and I'd still eat it."

Chapter Eighteen

Gigi

When Sheila's words registered, I doubled over.

She stood there, stone-faced. "You're laughing. I'm for real."

I held up my hand for mercy before going to one knee while the air returned to my lungs. Wiping my eyes, I managed to speak. "Woo girl, you are sick. I needed that."

I giggled a bit more as Sheila continued her Sitting Bull rendition. I waved her out of the master suite, catching my breath. "Let's just get this over with and bounce."

I took Sheila through the kitchen and we stopped at the tabletop well.

"G, can you give me that flashlight? I want to take a good look."

A long-handled, black flashlight sat cattycorner on the semicircular, granite island near the double sink. I passed it to Sheila and she admired the interior brickwork of the well for a long moment before speaking.

"G, this well is over a hundred years old. I heard that groundwater is better for you because it has lots of minerals in it from exposure to rock formations."

I huffed. "I don't know about all that, but I heard on the news that most tap and well water in the U.S. isn't safe to drink because of industrial pollution. So go on down there and get you a cupful of that stale water. I'll drive you to Grady."

Grady is Atlanta's local charity hospital. They actually have very good facilities, but overcrowding and underfunding make that difficult to know.

I'd seen my reflection at the bottom of the well and understood Sheila's fascination with the experience. Storie never looked down the entire time we chatted last week. I guess everybody has a different perspective on the same event; which would explain why truth is so hard to come by.

Sheila waved the light back and forth on the water's surface repeatedly, squinting. "G, come here a minute."

I shuffled over from the microwave where I took inventory of the kitchen gadgets the Killingsworths had left behind. "What's up, Sheila?"

Sheila gestured with her index finger for me to come closer to the glass top. "G, you see how the light disappears when I flash it to the left?"

"Yeah."

"I'm not sure, but I think it has something to do with how light refracts off water."

Sheila could have easily taken her degree in physics. The physics department did their best to persuade her but, in the end, her love for circuits, neural networks, and computer programming prevailed.

I know Sheila felt my puzzled energy because she started explaining without looking up. "Refraction is when a wave, like light or sound, bends as it passes from one medium into another of different optical density."

I stood there with my lips hanging. "Translation?"

Sheila looked up. "My bad, G. The translation is that when light passes from air to water, some of the light waves go into the water and some of them bend and go in a different direction."

My expression lightened. "Thank you for speaking English. Now tell me why any of that matters."

Sheila turned back to the well. "At first glance, it doesn't. But if you look closely you can see that, when I shine the light down the left side of the wall, it disappears before reappearing and bending off the water."

I clutched my clipboard, trying to keep my mind on inventory but frustrated that I couldn't. "Okay, I'll bite. So what does it mean?"

Sheila put the flashlight below her chin, pointed it upwards to illuminate her face, and responded in a bad Vincent Price accent. "It means that there's a hole in the side of the well. A big hole. Given how much light it swallowed at this angle, maybe as big as a door."

I checked my clipboard. "It doesn't say anything here about a room that leads to the well."

Sheila pulled the top of the clipboard and peeked down the list. "Well, what does it say?"

I snapped it back toward my chest and angled my neck. "Nothing. According to this, we've gone through every room in the house."

"G, you know these old houses have secret passageways and hidden rooms. For all we know, Captain Burns had a room where he hid a trunk full of confederate gold coins that he snatched from some Dixiecrat before the Union Army burned Atlanta to the ground."

Just then it clicked. "Hey, Storie did say she and Walters spent lots of time in some underground tunnels as kids and that she hated hauling water from this well."

Sheila retorted in a breathy manner. "Maybe they found a shortcut."

I ignored her suggestive tone. "Maybe. But how would we get there?"

Sheila went into engineer mode. "If the portal is here, then the entrance must be on the west side of the house."

I couldn't resist. "West-sy-eed!"

I enjoyed the comic relief, but Sheila had already developed a nose for the chase. She exclaimed. "You think I'm wrong, don't you?"

Ever since we were kids, all anybody had to do was dare Shelia to do something or call her 'chicken' and she would eat worms, jump off ladders, or race boys barefoot in the middle of the street before church with a new Easter dress on. But the absolute worst thing anybody could do is say they thought she was wrong when she thought she was right. Sheila would stop at nothing and go to the ends of the earth to vindicate her suspicions. When it turned out that she was, in fact, wrong, she would cross her arms, stare at the person, spin on her heels, walk away, and never mention it again.

We always made up after the fact, but I still had to tread lightly here. "I'm not saying you're wrong, I'm just saying I don't know about the feasibility of a room fifty feet underground with a door carved into the side of a well."

Sheila uncrossed her arms and quickly straightened them by her sides. "We'll just see, won't we Giovanni?"

Oh, it's Giovanni now? I followed Sheila out the kitchen because I knew the game was afoot. Or as we used to say back home, 'it's on'.

Chapter Nineteen

Gigi

We went traipsing all over the first floor looking for a secret passageway, trapdoor, or anything that would lead us to this hole in the bottom of the well.

Sheila stamped the floor and rapped walls incessantly, looking for hollow spaces and loose boards.

After her amateur sleuthing slowed down, she rested on the servant's stairwell. "G, it's got to be around here somewhere. In fact, I'm thinking that the opening would have to be about here to accommodate the slope of the diagonal between the outer wall of the house and the well."

I grimaced. "Uh, Sheila. English please."

"Oh, right. I'm just saying that if the entrance is inside the house, it's gotta be around this spot. Otherwise, you'd have to go straight down into the earth like you're sliding fifty feet down the bat pole with no way back up."

Physics prevailed again. Peering at the floor represented my nonverbal surrender to Sheila's reasoning. I absently stamped for hollow spots.

Sheila didn't appear to notice. "Man G, they must be balling to have marble around their butler's pantry."

"I know, right? Storie said…"

I stopped mid-sentence.

Sheila waited; then inquired. "Storie said what?"

By that time I was leaning against the staircase, adjacent to the butler's pantry. The butler's pantry displayed a combination of glass shelves on top and enclosed storage at the bottom. The white oak of the cabinetry seemed out of place against the knotted pine forming the staircase but, in real estate, whoever pays gets to pick.

I answered Sheila. "Storie said that they built this butler's pantry and laid these marble floors themselves. So…"

I didn't get a chance to finish the statement before Sheila had dropped to her knees, rummaging through the lower cabinets. No need to finish.

Sheila didn't look up. "I knew it, G. This area couldn't have been in the original design. It seems stuffed into the space."

Sheila pulled cans off the shelves and slid them. "It's here somewhere. Girl, look up top."

I instinctively screamed out. "Hey, don't scratch that marble. These floors cost serious money."

Sheila lifted her head. "My bad, G. You know how I get."

Boy, did I? I remember when we were in school, Sheila couldn't figure out a certain calculus problem during our sophomore year. So she went out and bought a dry erase board, nailed it to our dorm-room wall, wrote the problem, and stared at it for three days straight. While chit chatting or snacking, even when friends came by to visit, Sheila was polite but, if she wasn't being spoken to, she'd steal a glance at that calculus problem and make it clear that her interest for the moment lie on the board; not with us.

On the third night around two in the morning, Sheila rose up like Dracula with eyes wide open and exclaimed, "I got it!" All I can tell you is that, in a few seconds, she'd thrown off the covers, grabbed a marker, and solved the calculus problem without missing a beat. She startled me so badly with all that noise that it took thirty minutes for me to get back to sleep. Not her. After Sheila finished, she wrote 'Quite Easily Done' at the bottom of the board, climbed back into her coffin, and slept until noon.

As instructed, I began my search of the upper cabinet; knowing full well that this madness would not end until Sheila had exhausted every conceivable possibility. With Sheila, under these circumstances, resistance is futile and it would only drain me to try. So I thoroughly patted the interior surface, mentally checking off that interrogation question before it launched.

We are not friends because of the laughs we spend, but the tears we save. The phrase unfolded while thumbing through cups and saucers. In moments like this, my favorite poet helped me keep things in perspective. Instead of the outrageous demands of friendship, sometimes I would rather be kidnapped by a poem.

Sheila stood, brushing off her knees and thighs. “Anything?”

I was about to shake my head when I felt an oddly placed lever in the right posterior of the cabinet facing.

I reached across my body, pulled the lever down, and...

“G, you found it. I told you it was here!”

Chapter Twenty

Gigi

I did not believe my eyes. When I pulled the lever, an inlaid door popped out of the recess between the pantry and staircase. We both pried the door wide, then stared at each other. *Incredulous*, a term from one of Mrs. McFarland's 3rd grade vocabulary quizzes, was the unspoken word that came to mind when surveying Sheila's expression.

She narrowed it before speaking. "This is genius, Gigi. Even though I felt it should be in this area, I would've never imagined it'd be under the staircase."

I was still in mild shock, but forced myself to move into the doorway and pull the light switch cord. The single bulb illuminated the upper landing enough to see that there was a path leading down into the home's foundation.

Sheila followed me in. "G, do you see what I see?"

I affirmed. "Yeah, a stairway underneath the servant's staircase that goes down at the same angle. This is pretty amazing."

Sheila agreed. "For real. G, you got the flashlight?"

I looked down the hidden stairway and back at Sheila. "I know you're not suggesting that we...? That I...?"

Sheila stood firm. "Didn't Storie tell you something about going deeper? G, this is deeper. Let's just do it."

I inhaled, released, let my shoulders relax, flipped the flashlight on, and started down the stairwell.

I inched forward onto each step. At least there were handrails running the length of the descent. I could feel the moist rust flake underneath my palm. Better that than swatting at air.

"Sheila, I'm good on the Indiana Jones adventure. You can have this."

With her hand steadying my shoulder, Sheila retorted. "G, think of it as black women reclaiming what's ours. Full lips are called 'Angelina Jolie' lips. Full hips are called the 'J-Lo' butt. Black women never got ratified in that before other folks made it okay."

I didn't really see where she was going, but it did help to occupy my mind. "So?"

"So now we're going to be the tomb raiders and money train riders today. G, for all we know, there could be a zillion dollars worth of confederate doubloons stashed down here."

Doubloons were Spanish, but I had to admit that the history of the house made it plausible that something of value from that period could be hidden down here. And it could possibly be a chest of gold coins, whomever's picture happened to be stamped onto them. I swept with the flashlight and kept walking.

When we reached the bottom, I saw what I expected to see.

I stopped and Sheila queried. "What is it?

"What else? Ashes."

It was a cavern of ash, soot, and charcoaled logs consumed long ago by the fires of days gone by. It smelled like a dusty chimney with weak smoke. I fanned away the particles made visible by the flashlight and felt Sheila brush past me.

"G, shine the light over here. I think I smell something."

I followed her voice with the barrel of the lamp. "Me, too. But it smells stale." I made a bitter beer face and continued.

Sheila concurred. "I think it's water. Gigi, we're close. Walk with me."

As I did, I saw what had Sheila marching so fast. "You found the mouth of the tunnel."

"I won't say it G, because you already know."

I acquiesced. "I'm not going to lie. You did your Nancy Drew on this one."

Sheila stood with her chin elevated. "Gigi, you are indeed a woman of honor. I appreciate you acknowledging my superior position."

We lightly high-fived and entered the opening hewn in the side of earthen wall. The tunnel was an iron cylinder above and on both sides, with a well-worn dirt floor. It looked to be about forty feet long with ashes and soot ankle-deep the entire length. The smell of water grew stronger with every step so we figured the end of the corridor had to be the ledge next to the well.

My light caught something in the middle of the tunnel. "You see that?"

Sheila replied. "Uh-huh. Looks metal."

"That's just a piece of it. I wonder what it is."

We came to stand over the object and peered down at it under the light.

Sheila spoke. "Girl, it's a chest. I hope those confederate coins are rust-free in there."

We both laughed. The chest was wooden, about two feet square, and in relatively good shape for being underground near dampness. A lace-embroidered heart mounted by a ribbon sat etched in ivory on top.

I gave it a closer inspection. "Sheila, the metal thing is a latch. Help me get it open."

We bent down to pry at the lock before I grabbed Sheila's hand. "On second thought, the chest itself may be valuable. Let's just take it upstairs to make sure we don't damage it."

We squatted on either side to hoist the box and share the load. Ours eyes and smirks met as we rose.

Sheila remarked. "Well, one mystery solved. It's not gold doubloons."

Chapter Twenty One

Gigi

Good thing it wasn't full of coins. Tumbling down the dark, hidden stairwell crushed by a chest full of bullion doesn't sound cute. Even so, I think we would have taken the risk if it meant instantly doing away with our student loans.

I brought up the rear and couldn't help but feel something at my back. I kept turning around shining the light behind. Sheila complained about the periodic darkness in front, but I'm not down with getting snatched backwards by Michael Myers.

After shutting the inlaid door and breathing a sigh of relief, we brought the chest into the kitchen and set it on the glass top over the well. I shined the light onto the latch while we stooped to examine its condition.

"G, it doesn't look locked; just old. We can probably pop it open with little effort." Sheila made a flicking motion.

I agreed. "I think you're right. I wonder the last time somebody flipped that latch? And I wonder what's inside?"

Sheila nodded and straightened. I kept peering at the ivory heart. Sheila tapped me. "G, you should be the one to open it."

I stood up and faced her. She continued. "Look at where you are. You were right over this well when Storie told you to look deeper. You did that and went down into the well and found a tunnel. Now you're sitting here with an old chest with something in it. Who knows? You might even find Faithful Freddy in that box."

I swallowed. "But Sheila, if it wasn't for you, we wouldn't have found it."

Sheila held up her hand and stopped my speech. "Aunh, auh. No, Gigi. You are the *only* reason we're here. This is your moment."

I took a deep breath and flipped the latch. The lid of the chest sprang backwards like a reverse mousetrap. I recoiled into Sheila and the rear counter caught us both.

Sheila nudged me in the small of my back. "Handle your business, girl."

I swatted her hand. "Don't try to act like you weren't scared, too."

I scooted toward the chest and didn't see anything upon first glance. Inching, I spotted a weathered cover with the same heart and embroidering as the chest; except the cover had actual lace and the heart was adorned with decorative pink and crimson threading. I picked it up and placed it on the glass top.

Sheila slid over. "It's a book."

"Not exactly the treasure we were hoping for, huh?"

Sheila shrugged. "Not exactly. But it's the treasure we have, so let's take a look."

I cracked the cover and inhaled that 'ye olden' fragrance. The first page of the book contained the following words:

These Are The Lived Principles Of The Black Victorian Society
Established in London, England
1780
Dido Elizabeth Belle Lindsay, Founder
Chapter relocated to Atlanta, Georgia
1880

The linen paper had yellowed with age but the quality still endured. Each page contained the picture of a handsomely dressed black couple and a bold term written in calligraphy followed by a detailed, cursive explanation. The entries appeared to all be from a woman's point of view and the handwriting reflected female authorship.

Gingerly leafing, I heard Sheila's voice. "So you think it's a group diary or something?"

I shook my head. "I think it's more like a guidebook of some kind."

"A guidebook?" Sheila paused, then continued. "Well, the reason I said diary is because of the pictures and the entries written by women. Maybe this Black Victorian Society was a highfaluting women's club that got together for tea and crumpets."

"Maybe. But these key words at the top of the page make me think there's more order to this book than a diary would have. In fact, the concepts I saw… love, obligation, courting, duty…all seem to fit together. I bet when we read through them, they'll tell us everything we need to know."

Sheila sighed. "Okay, Gigi. But you know I'm a big picture person. So why do you think the Lord had us trudging down in that cave to find an old book?"

I returned her gaze. "If it's why I think, then we may have found the real reason for our website."

Chapter Twenty Two

Gigi

Now you have enough back-story to hear about the next time I saw Timo.

Okay. So I was out with Kenny at *Justin's*, P. Diddy's Restaurant on Peachtree NW. Why Atlanta named all these different streets Peachtree is anybody's guess, but Kenny ordered the twin lobster tails (one fried, one broiled) and I had the blackened catfish stuffed with shrimp, crab-meat, and three peppers. Scrumpy any night; especially that night. I figured since I would either leave there with a boyfriend or a 'could've been', I might as well enjoy my meal.

Kenny had been around for almost 3 months and my new system was working like a charm. See that little book we found turned out to be loaded with everything a woman needs to know to land and marry her man. They called it 'courting' back then. Sheila and I call it 'the business'. Everybody knew what time it was, men included. For instance, when a guy started courting a woman, he made a written declaration of his intentions. Yes, he actually put pen to paper and gave the formal letter to her parents, listing his qualifications and sincerity. That way everybody was clear on what was happening and cheating men were shamed in society as dishonorable. The common expectation was that the courting process would lead to marriage in an agreed upon timeframe.

Sheila and I could hardly sleep after we read it. The principles were sound, but it needed to be updated for the 21st Century. So we modified it ATL style and created *The Love Manual*. I'd been working out the kinks over the last few months and Kenny was my first real prospect.

"Kenny, I've really enjoyed getting to know you and I want to be as clear as possible about us."

Kenny put down his fork and dabbed the corners of his mouth with his napkin. "So have I. What's on your mind, Giovanni?"

I exhaled and began. "I like you and I think by the time we've spent together that you like me, too. But casual dating is not where I am right now. Instead I'm looking to date with the intention of marriage. We've both agreed that we want to be married and have children one day. The big question is whether we want that family to be with each other. There's only one way to find out: an exclusive, committed relationship where we only date each other with the goal of working toward marriage. Is that something you'd like to do?"

Kenny glanced from side to side, clutched for his water glass, and took two big gulps prior to speaking.

Before he could, I smelled a familiar fragrance and followed Kenny's eyes over my shoulder.

"Hi Giovanni. I never thought I'd see you again."

Timo was standing there looking all delicious like a Cadbury bunny. Sculpted in wrought iron, smiling like Taye Diggs, and wearing Italian silk, my temperature rose but I didn't let on.

"You two know each other?" Timo and I both turned toward Kenny.

I responded. "We do. At least we did."

Kenny stood to shake Timo's hand. "Have a seat. Something I ate is disagreeing with me. I'll be right back."

Kenny headed toward the men's room and Timo sat down. I started to protest but didn't give Timo the satisfaction.

"Admit it, Giovanni. You missed me."

"Missed a no-count brother who won't commit? I don't think so."

Timo leaned back in his chair, nodding. "No-count brother? Pretty good. How long did you rehearse that one?"

I nodded back, sarcastically.

Timo grinned like Big Bubba Sunshine. "What did you tell the man to make his stomach hurt?"

"Nothing I would ever tell you. In fact, I couldn't tell you because I would only say those words to a man."

Timo did a fake knife thrust before reaching at my water glass. I slapped at his hand, causing him to spill some on the table cloth. He snorted as he took a sip.

I raised my eyebrows. "You know what? I will tell you what I told him. Boys need to become men someday. I told him that I'm a real woman and not interested in dating around like a teenager. I think you call that 'kicking it'."

Timo made a steeple with his fingers and rested his nose on them.

"I also told him that I want us to date with the intention of working toward marriage."

Timo lowered his hands. "What did he say?"

"He didn't get a chance to say anything. Before he could, you barged up and interrupted the moment."

Timo chuckled. "Or provided an escape route."

"Whatever Timo. There are *some* real men in the world."

"Oh yeah? Well, what kind of car does he drive?"

"Timo, that is so materialistic. I wouldn't even expect *you* to be so base. But if you must know, he drives a Jaguar."

"Black with 'PEACE' on the license plate?"

"Yeah, how'd you know?"

"Cause he just tipped the valet and is turning right at the stop sign."

Timo pointed and I looked out the picture window in a slight panic.

As I turned back, the Maître d' approached palm in palm. "Excuse me, Ms. George? The gentleman asked me to convey his sincere apologies. He was not feeling well and had to leave suddenly. However, he has paid for your meal and invited your guest to dine in his stead."

The Maître d' returned to his post and Timo spread a napkin on his lap. "Great, 'cause I'm starving."

I started punching Sheila's number in when Timo spoke again. "Don't worry, I got you on the ride home."

The phone rang and rang with no answer. All I could hear was Timo's last line before the machine picked up. "He was real, alright. Real smart."

Chapter Twenty Three

Timo

I coasted in while Ricky was watching Conan O'Brien. "You'll never guess who I bumped into tonight?"

Ricky glanced over and returned to the set. "Must've been your little brother looking for his pants."

"Naw, for real. Guess."

"Man you know I'm not going to guess. Just tell me."

"Giovanni."

Ricky angled his head. "So did you speak or just watch her, licking your lips like Ted Bundy?"

"Did I speak? Bruh, this is your boy, Timo Barnett. You know I did my thang."

Ricky flipped off the television. "Aite. Run it down."

"Right, right. So I'm up in *Justin's* to get a bite and celebrate landing two second round draft picks."

Ricky leaned forward. "Word? Who'd you get?"

"Antoine Little and Devarius Jones."

"From Tech?"

I bobbed from side to side, dancing to an imaginary groove. "You know it."

Ricky slapped me five with a snap at the end.

I cleared my throat. "As I was saying, I strolled in to celebrate my conquest when who do I see sitting with this Poindexter in the corner?"

"Giovanni?"

"Exactly. I was feeling it dude, so I slid over behind her and just stood there. You know what I'm saying? That square was peeping me, but didn't say a word until she turned around to look."

"Good thing you started working out again. Because you were looking like Faizon Love for a minute."

I flexed at Ricky. "Shut up, Shawty Big Head."

I drawled out the first words. "As I was saying, that lame asked us if we knew each other then said he had to go to the potty…and left me alone with his woman. And you know me bruh; a wolf gotta eat."

"What about all that 'she hurt me' stuff you were laying down when you got here?"

"Ricky, Ricky, Ricky. It would be childish of me to hold a grudge this long. Do I look like a child?"

Ricky glanced at my pants and huffed. "I wouldn't call you a child, but I did think you were going to pass out after all that crying you did the first night. I had to call the boys to stand guard on suicide watch."

I threw a pillow at him. "You're sick in your mind. I admit it had me for a minute, but you're overboard with the exaggerations."

I straightened my shirt. "Anyway, I sat down and the head waiter slides over to say that her date paid the check and bailed."

"What?"

"Yeah, he dipped out of there faster than Rush Limbaugh chasing a wagon full of pills."

"Why?"

"That's just it, Rick. Not two minutes before I walked up, Giovanni told the man she wanted to date with the intention of getting married. That dude probably went to the bathroom to chuck his dinner."

Ricky shook his head. "I see you over there talking that stuff. Giovanni's a cute girl, man. But I know you know that. I'm just saying."

"Yeah, yeah, yeah. Well, since dude paid for the food already, why let it waste?"

Ricky smacked his teeth. "You're grimy, Timo."

"Whatever. If it's free, it's for me. So I'm trying to enjoy my dinner but Giovanni decides to torture me with her system to get a husband. I couldn't even taste my food because she's taking me through all the steps and stages of her little plan. And I had to hear it the whole time I was driving her home."

"Why did she tell you? I mean, if it's a female strategy to rope a man, it seems like she would keep it under wraps."

"I was thinking that, too, until she told me the answer." I held Ricky's gaze for a second without blinking. "She said I was nowhere on her list of possibles, so it doesn't matter if I know."

Ricky cupped his fist over his mouth. "She threw you in like a hand with no spades."

I bit my bottom lip. "We'll see."

Ricky rolled his eyes. "Oh, here you go. Always trying to scheme."

"I ain't scheming, Rick. Seeing Giovanni tonight reminded me of something."

"What?"

"That she and I have unfinished business."

"Oh, I thought seeing her reminded you of the other thing."

"What, Ricky?"

Ricky reached for the remote. "About how it felt to see Giovanni offer your old job to a Poindexter."

Chapter Twenty Four

Gigi

"Sheila, everybody's here. Let's get this show on the road."

The ladies were snacking on the fruit tray and chatting to catch up from the week.

Sheila emerged from the back with clicker in hand. "First let me thank you all for coming on this beautiful Saturday morning to give us feedback. The success of this depends on sisters sticking together and supporting each other. All we ask is that you keep an open mind and raise questions about any problems you see."

Mona responded. "Girl you know you can count on us. Gigi, you've got a nice place. I like these colors and the pineapples?" Mona dipped her head and breathed in a husky voice. "Juicy fruit."

That made the whole room laugh and set the tone. This Idea Party was the first gathering I'd had at my place besides Sheila and Diamond coming over. It's in the garden district and I have a few rosebushes in front of the porch on both sides of the steps. Not a castle, but comfortable and definitely enough for me. For now, it's home.

As to the attendees, Mona was a waitress at *Applebee's*. We met her one night when we first moved to town. All we had in those days was enough money to buy sodas and breadsticks. Mona used to feed us with her employee discount until we got on our feet. So every chance we get, we get together and treat her to a nice meal. Not that she needs it. That girl probably has more money stashed away than me and Sheila combined. But she's tight on a dollar. And she's certifiably insane, too.

Then there is her best friend Rita. We met Rita through Mona and the four of us became a 'Get-It-Girl' crew. Rita is the manager at *Dollar Rental Car* on Piedmont. So you know what that means when we road trip…convertible baby! Rita has a 5 year old, Carmen, who gets together with Diamond for play dates at least once a quarter. All of us are single and have had so many conversations about men that it made perfect sense for the four of us to form a focus group.

When Sheila finished the presentation, Mona and Rita sat silently. The twilight zone couldn't have been any stranger. I prodded. "So?"

Mona reached across the coffee table. "Girl, let me wet my throat before I tell you what I think."

Rita set her plate down to speak. "Well, I like the piece about the different kinds of men. You know that "Larry the Lover" character reminds me of Cleon Reynolds who always sits in the corner booth for lunch at your job, Mona. But let's face it girls, because of the shortage of men, they'll always have the upper hand in relationships."

I interjected. "Not true ladies, not true. Just sit still and answer this question in your mind: 'If all the women in the world were on one side of an island and all the men were on the other side, who could hold out the longest?"

Mona leaned back. "Do we even need to answer? You know those men would be running to us faster than sumo wrestlers at a Japanese barbeque."

I pointed at her. "And what if a man and woman are equally upset with each other? Who will make the first move to apologize?"

Rita conceded. "The man."

I hit them with one more. "But what if a man and woman have been seriously dating for years? The woman wants to get married but the man doesn't. What usually happens?"

Mona scooted to the edge of the sofa cushion. "Nothing. No marriage. No engagement. No nothing."

Rita added. "And to be honest, you're almost scared to bring it up because you might wake up the next morning and the guy has left the state. Especially in my case. And Sheila knows what I'm talking about. For us single moms, guys feel like they're doing us a favor by dating us. They think because we have kids, we're lonely and all we want is sex."

Mona raised her hand. "I want sex."

Everyone's belly shook. Mona continued. "No, for real, I do. And I know y'all do, too. But I just don't want it to be all about sex. I want a real relationship that's headed somewhere with a man that's not playing games."

Sheila seized the moment. "That's why we're launching "**T**he**L**ove-**C**ommitment.com."The site is for women who want to be married in the next two years or less to a man who is faithful and ready to commit."

Rita sighed. "Sheila, is this a dating site?"

"No ma'am. This is not match.com or Facebook. TLC is a site that encourages women to learn the love commitment system, teach each other, share their stories, and help each other in whatever stage their love commitment happens to be."

Mona threw up her hands. "You did say 'share stories', right? Like letting other women in my business? Naw, baby. Mona is like Homie. Mona don't play that."

Sheila swiveled. "I think Gigi should take it from here."

I took a deep breath before speaking. "Mona, the backbone of the entire system is women sticking together and supporting each other. Without that, nothing works."

Mona did a screeching noise. "You can stop right there, Gigi. Now I've been a lot of places and I've seen a lot of things, but I never recall seeing women stick together on anything; especially men. Am I right about it Rita?"

Rita fidgeted in her seat before responding. "I see your point, but I have seen women support women before."

Mona queried. "Where?"

"My sorority sisters. We only get together from time to time, but child I wouldn't have made it through some of the mess at school without them."

Sheila piggybacked. "Speaking of that, look at all the women's colleges where women come together and support each other. Here in Georgia we have Spelman, Brenau, Agnes Scott, and Wesleyan. But there're over fifty in the United States alone and hundreds worldwide."

I added to the fray. "And don't forget *Essence Magazine*. We all know business is business, but they are in the business of uplifting black women. They talk about our issues, our dreams, our struggles, and our triumphs. Girl, I haven't said anything about how much Oprah has done to help women everywhere. Mona, don't you believe for one minute that women can't stick together, because it's just not true. Look at us. Look at what we're doing right now."

Mona acquiesced. "Okay, to be perfectly honest, I have a better example than all of you. You know my sister is a Mary Kay Beauty Consultant. For the life of me, I couldn't figure out why a woman with a Master's Degree would run around town, burning good gas, doing facials, and selling make-up after working all day. So she finally convinced me to go to a Monday night meeting with her. Those women were in there talking about their successes and who they helped. I had to admit that I felt better when we left and that feeling carried over into the next day. So I went with her to their Seminar in Dallas and child, you would've thought Y2K really did wipe out all the bad credit. Those women were jumping and screaming and dancing and crying. I couldn't blame them, though. There were so many furs, diamonds, and pink Cadillacs being given away, I felt like I was at the Playa's Ball."

I concurred while we giggled. "You got it, Mona. Those women are up in there handling business. And that's exactly what The Love Commitment is: Grown Women's Business."

Mona had softened, but still wasn't convinced. "That's the thing. I see the incentives in Mary Kay: I get respect, I get appreciated, I get treated fairly, I get promoted, and I get paid. I'm good. But Gigi, I don't see the incentives here beyond the hope of getting a man."

I closed my eyes and smiled. "We all listen to WIIFM."

Everyone in the room grimaced before I explained. "What's In It For Me?"

Rita and Mona high-fived. I continued. "I'm glad we're all on the same page. What's in it for you is the same thing that's in it for all of us: we get a loving, committed, relationship that results in marriage, family, children, and happiness. But the catch is, if we help each other get it, then we all get it. But if we don't help each other get it, none of us get it."

Rita moaned. "Gigi, I was at 'Sisters in Spirit' meeting last week and while Tricia was teaching she said we are our sister's keeper. I didn't fully know what she meant until this moment. Sheila, it's not just single moms that need to stick together, but all women."

Sheila put her hand on Rita's shoulder. "I know girl. Last time I talked to Tricia, she was telling me to be a sister to all. This is a big part of what she means. I admit it's hard to get past the competition idea in everybody's mind, but what we've got here will literally change the world."

Mona stood up. "Alright, alright. I'm in. And while I'm at it, I might as well go back to school, subscribe to *Essence*, and join Mary Kay. Now start from the beginning and tell me how this Love Commitment thing works again."

Chapter Twenty Five

Timo

D.C. led with a little joker. "That's how you pull trumps, oy. If you start with a nine, you're just wasting spades."

Luke followed suit with a three. "See you need to watch your mouth. I minored in Spades at FAM. It's called 'fishing', D. Fishing. If you don't have enough trumps in your hand to drain all the spades, you fish to let your partner get in if he can."

I glanced across the table at Ricky and then broke in. "Uh Luke, you can coach D.C. when the hand is done. By the way, where I'm from that's called talking across the board. Can we get those three books?"

Luke retorted in a learned southern drawl. "Man, shoot. I know we're beating y'all like they beat Denzel in *Glory*, but you don't have to make up rules Timo."

D.C. laughed. "I'm saying, Timo. Even if we gave y'all three books, you still wouldn't have board."

D.C. laid down the rest of his cards and they were all winners. He did the rattler strike motion and Luke mirrored it. "We might as well talk about your big plan to get back at Giovanni. If you ask me, you're being childish and this shows how wounded you really are."

I tossed in my hand. "Nobody asked you dude-with-no-love-life."

"No love life? Man I got women standing in line waiting."

"Yeah, waiting at the police station to file a restraining order."

D.C. shook his head. "Childish."

Ricky tossed his hand in, too. "For real Timo, what's the plan here? You've kept it under lock and key all week. So let's hear it."

I pushed my chair back from the table. "No doubt. But first let me tell you Giovanni's system."

I stood up. "After she meets a dude she likes, she makes small talk and slides in three quick questions: (1) Who are you? (2) What do you want out of life? and (3) What are you up to now?"

Luke interlocked his fingers, looking up and to the left. "So what answers does she want?"

I shrugged. "Beats me. All I know is that she says she doesn't have time to waste on men who aren't serious. According to her, she's only open to going on a date if you pass that test."

D.C. couldn't contain himself. "What did you do to that girl, Timo? Now we all have to pay for your sins."

Ricky had kept quiet until then. "So what's next?"

I frowned. "What do you mean?"

"What's next in the system?"

Luke seconded. "Yeah, Timo. Give up the goods."

I recomposed. "She said she would get the answer to every question and end the encounter shortly after. If he passes, she'll give him her number so they can set up a date."

Luke scratched the back of his neck. "What's up with all the formality?"

"She said something about business being business. To tell you the truth, I really don't know. But to answer your question Ricky, Giovanni was real particular to say that the first date should be at least one week after the initial encounter."

Ricky moaned. "How come?"

"Now this one I guess I can take the blame for. She said she spent too much time with me too fast without thinking through what I said I wanted."

"Which was?" Ricky gestured with his fingers.

"Giovanni didn't ask me any of these questions at first. But when she did, I was straight up. I told her I wanted to build my career and start my own business as a financial planner for NFL athletes."

D.C. reached for a soda. "What about family?"

"I told her I wasn't ready for a family yet and I couldn't even think about that until my business got off the ground. She said she could respect that and we kept it moving."

Ricky rubbed his chin. "So what happens on this first date?"

"The questions get deeper. Your past relationships, what happened, when, how far along, the works.

Luke frowned. "Man, when women start asking about the past, it's a turn-off for me."

"Patterns." We all observed Ricky. "She's looking for patterns."

I smirked. "Okay Sharp Eye Washington. What kind of patterns?"

"Patterns of behavior. Patterns of relationship sabotage. Patterns of self-sabotage. Basically, she's trying to figure out if anything about the guy causes his relationships to consistently fail."

D.C. wiped his mouth and nudged. "Like what, Rick?"

"Like lying, cheating, selfishness, immaturity, low self-esteem, or just plain not being ready to commit like broke Jerry McGuire over there sleeping on my sofa. It could be any issue that's unresolved in his life."

I snatched the imaginary microphone. "Thank you Tyra Banks. Whose side are you on anyway?"

Ricky waved me off. "I'm just saying I understand what she's doing. I saw a show one time where this dude came clean and said he couldn't figure out why he would push away women who were madly in love with him."

Luke scrunched his neck. "How did they look?"

"Beautiful. They brought two of them onto the stage and these women were dime pieces on any day of the week. What came out is that the brother had intimacy issues that stemmed from commitment anxiety."

We all threw up our hands. I spoke first. "Rick, the women are already out to get us. We don't need you psychoanalyzing us like Hannibal Lecter."

"Bruh, the dude confessed that he intentionally pushed them all away because he was afraid that if they got into his heart, he would have to commit."

D.C. brought in reinforcements. "So the man wasn't ready to commit. What's wrong with that?"

Ricky flattened his lips. "What's wrong with it is he was 42 years old."

D.C. followed. "But we've all been there. 42, 22, 92…if the man wasn't ready, he wasn't ready."

Ricky uppercut us with his response. "But he was ready to have sex."

Gut punch. I fired back. "Rick, sounds like that guy on the show was you. I remember at least three young ladies waiting in the lobby of Gibbs Hall for you on different occasions; until the R.A. kicked them out. You had to hide in the room for a week until they finally had their last cries and gave up. So now you're all rehabilitated?"

"I'm trying to be."

"Man, you haven't dated a woman in four years. For all we know, you're an axe murderer waiting to happen."

Ricky tightened his jaws. "It's obvious that I'm not the only one with commitment issues Timo 'cause, if you didn't have any, your girl wouldn't be crusading to replace you."

Luke stood up muscle popping. "He's got a point, Timo." D.C. joined in.

Ricky added. "Bruh, if you're finished changing the subject and masking your pain, can you tell us what happens next?"

I snapped. "Why are you so interested?"

"Because I'm glad the sister is getting systematic. I teach kids all day and the only way I know that they're learning is using assessments."

D.C. mumbled. "I hate tests."

"We all do when we're not prepared. But when we study and we like the subject, a test is just a chance to show what we know. Since we all like women, then you can figure out that for the last four years I've been studying for my test while Timo has been planning to cram. So what's after all these intro dates?"

I let that last comment slide and answered. "What comes next is either a phone call where she tells the guy she doesn't think they're headed in the same direction or a face to face where she proposes..."

Luke cut me off like a chipmunk on Mountain Dew. "Proposes?"

"Can you let me get it out rapper-on-crack?"

I resumed. "...where she proposes that they take a couple of months to learn each other and see what the real possibilities are."

D.C. gasped. "You mean she wants you to give up your other honeys? After three weeks? Man, I'm like Luda. Get back, back. You don't know me like that!" Luke shimmied his shoulders on beat.

I lowered my hand. "Sit down Hammer. At that point, she said she's not asking to be exclusive. Since it's an exploration phase, I guess you get a chance to weigh the person against other people of interest before you make a decision. To do that, you need to interact with other options."

Ricky exhaled. "So is that the date Giovanni was on the night you saw her at *Justin's*?"

"Nope. She was two months ahead of that date when I saw her. The 'Let's-See' Date is Phase 2. Giovanni was trying to initiate 'Phase 3' with Poindexter."

Luke laughed. "Phase 3? Sounds like another card game that you'd be bad at."

I crossed my arms. "Naw bruh. None of us can play this game. Wait until you hear what I haven't told you."

Chapter Twenty Six

Gigi

I pulled up beside Captain Burns' grave and hurried inside to flip the lights for my 9am appointment.You know I don't normally do this, but this is my first 3.3 million dollar listing. So I can't let just anybody have access to the property. And by 'just anybody', I'm talking about the real estate agents. But this situation had another special element: the buyer making the appointment didn't have an agent. His secretary phoned my office yesterday and told me he wanted to keep the transaction confidential. If during our meeting he felt comfortable, he would ask me to represent him as a dual agent. In other words, if I close the deal, I'd get to keep the whole $200,000 commission. I made sure to wear my black and cream pinstripe suit and hit Starbucks on the way in.

I didn't know much about him. All I knew was that he was a professor at Emory. Many corporate professionals become professors late in life to share their knowledge and have time to enjoy their wealth. I hadn't done my usual prequalification letter due to the short notice but, in a way, we were both interviewing each other.

I heard the chime and opened the door with my right hand extended. "Dr Haynes?"

My voice trailed off as names and memories flooded my mind. He shook my hand and spoke. "I see you still like your caramel macchiato."

I peeked at my left hand and returned my gaze. "Eric?"

"Hello Giovanni. It's so good to see you." Eric continued to shake my hand softly. "Beautiful is an understatement. May I come in?"

I didn't know if he was talking about me or the house. I didn't care. I stepped aside, still processing the moment. Eric released his hold.

I put my hand on my hip. "So *you're* Dr. Haynes?"

Eric held up his hands, palms out. "Yes, but let me explain before you say anything."

I tilted my head to the side. He continued. "I knew things between us ended before they even got started. It was all my fault and I understand completely if you never want to see me again. Just hear me out and, if you want me to leave, I'll go."

Well at least he got one thing right: he *was* wrong for dumping me. But since he began with honesty, I took a sip of my caramel macchiato and remained silent.

Eric seized the moment. "I should have never let things get as far as they did. But I really fell for you and didn't want to let you go. I wrestled with it for weeks before I finally mustered up the courage to do what was best for us both."

I couldn't take it. "Lead me on and dump me?"

"No. End it before we got intimate. If that had happened and things didn't work out, you'd hate me and I'd hate myself."

I took a slower sip. He kept going. "So the most honorable thing I could think to do was end it if we'd ever have a chance of being together in the future."

I grimaced and pulled the trigger. "Being together? Us? So you concocted this scheme to get some play? Who was the lady on the phone? Do you even have a secretary?"

I took a breath and he squeezed in. "Yes to everything you said. I didn't think I would ever see you again, but I literally could not stop thinking about you. When I opened a book, you were there. When I sat in a lecture, you were there. I would take breaks in Starbucks in hopes of running into you. I didn't know what I'd say if we ever met, but I had to try."

He paused. My heart stopped. He resumed. "So after I graduated,

I had three offers but only one in Atlanta. Emory's a great school with a top notch African American Studies Department, but the deciding factor was a shot to be with you."

Then my heart dropped into my shoes. Maybe it was the house and the wish I made after seeing Storie's rug, but it sounded like my wish had come true.

I couldn't speak or think. He could. "The lady on the phone is not my personal secretary, she's the department secretary. I told her our story and she helped me arrange this meeting. As you've probably guessed by now, I have about as much chance to buy this house as I did when you met me. But if you'll let me, I'd like to pick up where we left off and make it up to you."

I stared at Eric's expression, turning his words over in my mind. His earnest appeal made up for the postponement of my commission, but I'm not Renee Zellweger...he didn't have me at 'hello'. I placed my macchiato on the window ledge and crossed my arms.

Chapter Twenty Seven

Gigi

When a tiny bead of sweat formed on his forehead, I turned the knife. "Just like that, Eric? You think you can waltz in here like Cary Grant because you say you're ready now?"

His eyes stayed on mine. "I'd hoped it was more like Sydney Poitier, but I get your point. Whatever I have to do, I'm willing."

"Oh really?" I looked him over and prepared for him to hit the door faster than Deion Sanders.

I thought about taking his car keys to make sure he heard me out. Instead I raised my eyebrows. "We'll see. I need you to know that we can't 'pick up where we left off'. It's been over five years since the last time I saw you. Five years, Eric. I was looking for a boyfriend then. Now I'm looking for a serious commitment moving toward marriage. So what are your intentions?"

Eric moved closer. "I wouldn't be here if those weren't my intentions. And since '5' is the number of grace, I'm praying that you can find it in your heart to give me one last try."

Sheila had mentioned the divine number thing before, but I doubt that she would accept this coming from Eric. "I'm not looking to date around or play games, Eric."

"Giovanni, I'm not seeing anyone and I wouldn't be here if I were. The only people in my life are my students and it's really not good for a man to be alone."

I nodded. "I agree. I also don't think that it's good for things to move too fast."

He nodded. “I agree with that.”

“Good. So that’s why I’ve decided that I don’t want to have sex until I’ve made a true love commitment.”

Eric shrugged his shoulders. “I absolutely agree. Sex too soon can complicate things. Lying on our backs and watching the stars will keep us until the time is right.”Was this guy reading my mind or had he taken a peek at my playbook? Whichever one it was, he said all the right things. I closed the distance, closed my eyes, and wrapped my arms around his neck.

Timo

Luke walked over and stooped to get in my face. “You say no cookies until the love commitment? Naw playa, I got to get mine from beginning to end, end to beginning. Know what I’m saying?”

D.C. echoed the sentiment. “I feel you Luke. Man, for real. You can get sick like that. Matter of fact, I think that’s how Marvin Gaye died.”

D.C. sung into his fist. “Bay-ay-ay-bee-ee, I got sick this morning…”.

We all joined the chorus. “..and when I get that feeling…”.

When the laughter subsided, D.C. questioned me. “So Timo, what did you say when she told you about not having sex?”

“Man, I just kept my eyes on the road, giving her the gasface. I didn’t even understand what she was saying. If we’re not being intimate, what does it mean to be in a relationship?”

Luke interjected. “Friend Zone.”

I concurred. “Exactly. I don’t need anymore friends. I need those ends.”

D.C. pointed. “I’m telling you, Timo. Besides, there’re plenty of women out there. If one says 'no', the next one will say 'yes'. It's all about the numbers. If you shoot enough arrows, you're going to hit something."

Ricky attacked from the side. "In your case, you're going to catch something."

D.C. watched Luke snicker. "What are you laughing at Itchy Scratchy?"

D.C. resumed his point. "Y'all think I'm playing, but I'm dead serious. Man, this a major threat to the game."

Luke agreed. "On the strength, it really is a true hater move."

Ricky muffled. "Maybe the game needs to be changed."

D.C. objected. "Don't hate the player."

Luke added. "And please don't hate the game."

I looked at Ricky and slumped my shoulders. "Dawg, the talk shows got to you? You been drinking the Kool-Aid, bruh? I knew I shouldn't have left you up watching those infomercials."

Ricky retorted. "Man, I'm just saying, it's time for something different." He looked over at D.C. and Luke. "Aren't you two tired of running women?"

They cut their eyes at each other before responding and soul-shaking. "Not really."

I queried Ricky. "Why are you Bill Cosby all of a sudden?"

"Timo, I work with these kids every day. Most of them are growing up without fathers and getting picked off by the thousands. And I know what it means for a man to be in the home. My dad wasn't perfect, but he was there. Neighborhoods with dads at home don't have drug dealers standing on the corner. That's a fact."

"I hear you Rick. But what? We're all supposed to get married to solve the problem?"

"Not all of us. But the ones that want to lay up and make babies definitely need to."

I bowed my neck. "I don't have any babies."

"Not now. But that's what naturally follows sex."

D.C. intervened. "Rick, stop trying to jinx a brother. I keep Jimmy strapped up tight."

Ricky shot back. "Plastic bags do burst."

D.C. covered his private parts. "Hey, I'm with Timo. Whose side are you on anyway?"

"The side of these kids we abandon and the women we leave to raise them. Our kids and our women deserve better than that."

Luke nodded. "I can't argue with you Rick, but it's still a hater move."

I wanted to be mad. Instead I was torn because I couldn't shake the feeling that telling the guys about Giovanni's system had backfired and somehow worked in her favor. I stood there beleaguered by my thoughts, like a snitch that had been cheated out of his paycheck.

Chapter Twenty Eight

Timo

Our 20mph speed was thanks to a city bus that had decided to straddle both lanes for the last half mile. That made Ricky's provocation all the more annoying.

"Whatever Ricky."

"Timo, I'm not lying. Luke and D.C. said they saw her hugged up with some dude at Barnes and Noble the other day."

I smirked. "And what were Luke and D.C. doing in Barnes and Noble? Can those fools even read?"

"Bruh, they go there to pick up women."

I scoffed. Ricky continued. "They meet lots of women trolling around the fiction section. Luke pretends to have an argument with D.C. about the meaning of some popular romance novel and, to settle it, asks a nearby woman for her opinion. According to them, they never leave without each getting a set of digits."

I adjusted the rearview mirror. "Guess it goes to show that courage and a wing man go a long way."

"I'm telling you. So yesterday they were running that Wing-T offense when they saw Giovanni and some dude over in the soft chairs, leg to leg, giggling. Luke said dude had his arm around her the whole time."

"So? What do I care?"

Ricky didn't answer and the silence lingered. I hung a left into the Buckhead Library parking lot and shut the car off.

Ricky unbuckled his seatbelt. "Why are we stopping here?"

"I need to use the computer real quick. Don't worry. We have plenty of time to make it."

Ricky coaches a co-ed soccer team of 8 year olds and I was making good on my promise to attend one of the games.

"Well hurry up. You know I like to scout the competition for next week. What's so urgent anyway?"

I found an open terminal, entered my card number, and typed in the web address: www.TheLoveCommitment.com.

Ricky stood by my chair. "What's that?"

"That's the site Giovanni told me they were taking live the night I drove her home. I had a strong urge to see if they did it."

"Looks like they did. But who is *they*?"

"Giovanni and…".

I rose and walked past Ricky with a grin pasted onto my face. "… Sheila!"

Sheila came through the doors being dragged by a small child headed for the kiddie section. "Well, well, well. If it isn't Timo Time Bandit."

I kept my composure. "What's up Sheila? I like those shades. And hey Diamond. Girl, you are getting so big. Pretty soon you'll be playing on Mr. Ricky's soccer team."

Sheila glanced over at Ricky. He spoke before she could. "Hey Sheila."

Sheila pulled her shades onto the bridge of her nose. "Ricky."

He smiled and looked at Diamond. "Let me show you my favorite book when I was your age."

Ricky took Diamond's hand and led her to the bean bags near the Curious George books. Right on. A true wingman.

Turning back to Sheila, I dove in. "So who is this I hear your girl is hugged up with these days?"

"Oh, so you're hawking now Timo?"

"Naw, I'm just asking. My sources told me they saw her with some L7 the other day and I was concerned."

"And why is that?"

"I'm sure she told you about the night I had to keep her from running barefoot after that square who left her at *Justin's*. A person can't take too many blows to their dignity. Prince says even doves have pride."

Sheila scoffed and rejoined. "She told me. Now I can tell her that one whiff of her perfume put Deputy Dog back on the case."

I made my lips vibrate. "You tried me then. Timo B. ain't no bloodhound, Boo Boo. This information came to me."

"Uh-huh. I see those tears in your eyes. But I don't feel sorry for you because you had your chance."

Dead end. Different approach. "You must like this new dude. Is he your cousin or something?"

Sheila pursed her lips. I noticed.

"He's nobody to me. In fact, as trifling as I think you are, I prefer you over him."

Pay dirt. "So what did he do to you?"

"Nothing really. Nothing besides I just don't like him."

"Tell me about it?"

Sheila put her shades on her hip, "For somebody who's not a bloodhound, your nose is sure wide open. What's it to you?"

I had to think fast. "Giovanni told me that night that I wasn't marriage material. I admit I'm interested in knowing what she's into these days."

"I see. Ego rides again. You guys are all the same. When women are throwing themselves at your feet, you couldn't care less. But as soon as another brother tries to holler, you're all Leonardo DiCaprio in *Titanic*."

"I never lost interest in Giovanni."

"But you never stepped up either."

I gritted my teeth. "She changed the plan along the way."

Sheila moved closer to my face. "She had to call an audible, Timo. You were going to run the same play the whole game."

She had me there. I stuck out my fist. "Game recognizes game."

She bumped.

"Now are you going to ignore your intuition about this dude or tell me the low-low on him?"

Sheila crossed her arms and looked me over. "Sit down."

While filling me in, she paused a few times to watch Ricky read to Diamond. Something about their play gave Sheila a serious expression.

"That's as much as I know. She keeps me in the dark on this guy, too."

"Sounds like a cool dude. Hope they work out."

Sheila cut her eyes at me and stood as Ricky and Diamond returned. "Did you have a good time, Baby?"

"Yes ma'am. Mr. Ricky is a funny storyteller."

"Did you say thank you?"

Diamond rushed to Ricky and squeezed him tightly. "Thank you."

Ricky stroked her hair. "You're welcome sweetheart. Anytime."

I touched Sheila's arm. "So what about this love commitment site you all built?"

Sheila squinted. "How do you know about that?"

"Giovanni told me the night Bullet Bob Hayes ran out on her."

"Well, it's been live for a week, but we're already getting major traffic."

"How?"

"We hit Facebook and Twitter. In a matter of hours, we had 20,000 hits. I had to buy more server space to make sure the site didn't crash."

"Interesting."

Sheila replaced her shades. "Gigi's going to announce it Monday when she goes on *Atlanta Live* to talk about *The Love Manual*."

This time I squinted. "The what?"

Sheila grabbed Diamond's hand. "Honey, the website is a pre-game speech. *The Love Manual* is the playbook."

Sheila turned and spoke over her shoulder with Diamond in tow. "Have a good game, Ricky."

By the way Ricky watched her exit the sliding doors, it was clear that the game had already begun.

Chapter Twenty Nine

Timo

Sheila left a bitter-sweet taste in the library. Guess I got stuck with the bitter.

"So you're playing Mr. Mom now, Ricky?"

"Diamond is cool people."

"Yeah, right. Not to mention, there was nothing but heat between you and Sheila."

"Just being polite, Timo."

"Any more polite and you all would've needed a room."

'What are you talking about?"

"I saw her eyes lingering; especially when Diamond hugged you. I'm telling you bruh, you're 'grade A' sirloin on the Daddy Day Care tip."

"Sheila is looking delectable these days but, to be honest, that ready-made family is not something I'm trying to do."

"Humph. I thought you'd be telling me most women have kids so guys should accept it."

"While it is true that the age of the average new mom is 25, I'm still not trying to hear it."

"Ricky, how and why do you know that?"

"I read, bruh. Ever heard of *USA Today*? Plus it was on *CBS News* two years ago. What planet are you from?"

"Obviously not yours." I backed out of the parking lot and continued. "So Mr. 'I read', if you're so enlightened, why don't you accept the fact that lots of women our age have kids and so crossing women off for that reason doesn't make any sense?"

"I can't. I've argued that point in my head a thousand times. My only answer is that I always grew up expecting to date and marry a woman that had no kids."

"But what if you were the one with kids?"

"Honestly, I'd still want a woman with no kids."

I stopped at the light and shook my head. "Kind of hypocritical, don't you think?"

"Absolutely. But I have another reason on top of the kid on that one."

"What?"

"Baby Daddy."

I shot back. "Baby Daddy? You do realize you would be a Baby Daddy, too, in that scenario?"

"Yep. But I'd be a sane Baby Daddy. Not some clown who decides to kill his ex and her new man because he can't live with the thought of another dude raising his child. No, thank you."

"Rick, you're sliding down a slippery slope."

"Look, I admit I have a hang-up with the family in a box. I also fully acknowledge my past issues. I've lied and cheated on women. I'm over that. All I'm asking for at this point is a woman with a good mind who takes care of herself with no kids. Is that too much?"

"Naw. But you find who you find. And you could end up bypassing a good woman for an idea that might not exist for you."

"Everybody has standards, Timo."

"For sure. But since when is a child a problem for you?"

"To be totally transparent, if another man had that kind of connection with my wife, I'd be a little insecure."

"A little?"

"Okay, a lot."

"I feel that Rick. I guess we all could. But the way you were giving it to us the other night about sex and raising these kids, it's just surprising to hear you say this."

"I understand. I still think those things. But if I have my rathers, I'd rather meet a young lady and start from scratch." Ricky looked out the window. "Can we change the subject?"

I saw Ricky needed a break, but he was usually the one that had me on the ropes. I fought off the dark side and relented. "Okay, to what?"

"To you and Giovanni."

We pulled into the park and sat in the gravel. "There is no me and Giovanni."

"So you say. But this morning I mentioned that the boys saw one of your old girls and you almost wrecked your car to find a computer."

"Whatever. I just wanted to check something out."

"Yeah, something about her. In college we used rib each other about seeing old girlfriends. But I never saw you breaking the speed limit afterwards. Tell me the real, dude."

I white-knuckled the steering wheel at ten and two o'clock and took my time before speaking. "Revenge."

"For what?"

"For humiliating me, that's what."

I looked over at Ricky, then returned my gaze straight ahead. "Man, I had to rebuild my self-esteem after I came to your place with my clothes in garbage bags. She took that from me and I'm not letting her off the hook."

Ricky put down the window. "What's that supposed to mean?"

"It means I'm going to humiliate her the same way she humiliated me…only worse."

"How?"

"By winning her back then dumping her the way she dumped me. But first I have to figure out a way to come between her and the professor."

"Timo, this is crazy. Only love can make a man say things like this."

"I agree. I love her more than I've ever loved any woman. But there's a thin line between love and hate."

Chapter Thirty

Gigi

"I'll have two eggs, scrambled, with cheese and wheat toast."

"Anything to drink?"

"Orange juice."

"Coming right, up."

The server took our menus and punched in the order. Sheila seemed distracted. Diamond colored on the kid's placemat and completed the word search with a yellow crayon.

I nudged. "What's up?"

Diamond intercepted the moment. "Mommy, can I play soccer?"

Sheila fidgeted with the salt shaker. "I think so, Sugar. Mommy will look into it."

I waited until she placed it back in the holder before interrogating. "Okay, you're as quiet as a church mouse and now the cartoon queen wants to be a sports star. What gives?"

Sheila started to pick up the salt shaker again before meeting my eyes. "We saw Timo and Ricky at the library on the way over here."

"And?"

"And Ricky coaches soccer. He and Diamond hit it off."

"That wasn't the 'and' I was referring to, but it's a start. Keep going."

"And Timo wanted to know about you and Eric."

"What? How did he...?" My tone got deeper. " Sheila?"

"He already knew."

"How?"

"How should I know? He knew about the love commitment site, too. I wonder how he found out about that?"

I sipped my juice and confessed. "Alright. I pushed his face in it the night Kenny ran out on me. I was furious and Timo was the perfect target for my redirected rage. He deserved it."

"Could be. But now Timo and Ricky are in the loop so we've got to be more careful."

"Careful about what? And what's all this talk about Ricky?"

"Mommy said Mr. Ricky is a nice man."

Sheila looked at Diamond with the shushy-face. My cheeks broadened. "She did? Well, that explains everything."

Sheila casually reached for a piece of toast. "Explains what?"

"Explains why you're such a lady whenever Ricky is mentioned."

Sheila deliberately spread the apricot jelly in long strokes for emphasis. "I'm not into friends of best friend's ex-boyfriends. Besides, not too many men are into single moms."

"That's not what it sounds like to me. All I hear out of you and Diamond is Ricky, Ricky, Ricky. He must have been into both of you because you're both into him."

Sheila dropped her eyes. I pounced. "I knew it!"

"But G, I don't want to be."

"Why not? Because he teaches Social Studies?"

"Girl, don't remind me. No, as crazy as it sounds, I can give him a pass on that. But Diamond and I are still bonding and I don't have time for a man gobbling up all my attention. You know men are like children."

I nodded. "Child, if you don't give them your undivided attention on every single thing, they're liable to throw a tantrum and tear up the whole house."

Sheila high-fived. "And I don't need any more kids right now."

"I hear you girl. But there are two flavors in nature that are scarce; and men like them both."

"What?"

"Sweet and salty. So you must have dished out some heavy doses this morning on Pretty Ricky."

"I didn't have time to. Your ex was sweating me about you and Dr. Humanities. He said something about you all snuggling in public. As horny as you both are, I had no problem believing it."

"You didn't tell him anything, did you?"

"What's to tell? You've always kept Eric a closely guarded secret. All I know is name, rank, and serial number."

"Why did you tell him anything at all?"

"Because it was obvious that he still has it bad for you and I wanted to see him salivate."

"Uh-huh. And it had nothing to do with you disliking Eric?"

"I admit, that broke professor thing is cliché and will never be attractive, but I can get over that. His similarities to Steve are tougher, but still not impossible to get beyond. Yet, there's something about him that I can't quite put my finger on."

"He's sweet, he's considerate, he's well-educated, he's gainfully employed, and he's committed to me. What's not to like?"

"I know. That's what has me worried. He's too perfect."

Chapter Thirty One

Timo

Sunday is when the fellas and I unwind and improve our sports knowledge by catching a few games. D.C. was the first to speak when Ricky came through the door. "Man Rick, why do you go to that tiny church and what are y'all doing 'til two o'clock in the afternoon?"

Ricky tossed his keys on the end table and plopped down. "What are you two doing here?"

Luke answered. "Man we came over to keep Timo company."

I added. And watch the game."

Luke rejoined. "That, too."

Ricky sighed. "Well if you must know, I go to church for the Word, not the theater. Pastor Tibbs has a strong message about doing God's work in the community. The spirit is high and sometimes we lose track of time."

D.C. jested. "Smells like you lost track of your deodorant."

I couldn't resist. "Naw, that's the smell of the Spirit."

Luke jumped on the dog pile. "Rick, y'all must have had some stankin' church today."

We held our stomachs because they ached. Ricky chuckled sarcastically when he lifted his elbows and saw the sweat rings under his arms. He tried to change the subject. "So who's playing?"

The laughter stopped abruptly, then restarted with a fury. We screamed like Raj, Dwayne, and Rerun on *What's Happening*. Ricky unbuttoned his dress shirt. "I know it's the playoffs. I just don't know which game is on."

I'd calmed down enough to speak. "Nice try, bruh. It's the NBA finals and Atlanta is up 2-1. They've never won the ring and haven't had a decent team since Dominique Wilkins."

Ricky folded his shirt across his lap. "Don't you mean Jacques Wilkins?"

Luke shook his head. "Jacques? I never heard of no Jacques Wilkins."

Ricky clasped his hands. "Even though Dominique played at the University of Georgia, he was born in Paris and his first name is Jacques. His dad was stationed there as an officer in the Air Force. Dominique is his middle name but, if you think about it, it's French, too."

Ricky had done it again. The inevitable question was asked by D.C. this time. "Rick, how do you know that?"

I braced myself for Ricky's pat response. "Dude, I read."

D.C. grabbed some chips. "No doubt. Say, we have a few minutes before the game starts so let me ask you this: Timo told us about the five types of men according to Giovanni and Sheila. But do you know about the five types of women?"

I reached for a handful of nuts and sat back. "You gotta hear this, Rick. Go ahead and drop that science, D."

"With pleasure." D.C. wiped his mouth and began. "The first type is called the Lazy Susan. I mean this broad is lay-zee. She doesn't want to cook, she doesn't want to clean, and she doesn't want to go to work. She wants to sleep all day and get treated like a movie star all night. She has no grind whatsoever but puts everything into her looks and her nightlife."

Ricky queried. "So why would you even be with her in the first place?"

Luke fielded this one. "Easy. She's super-fine and a super-freak. She could teach classes on how to satisfy a man."

D.C. took over. "Right. And that's good in the beginning. But soon those looks and sex start sucking the life out of you. Man I had this one girl, she looked so good I got suspicious about why she chose me. Real talk. I do alright, but I knew she could have been with a true baller; so why me? After a while, I figured it out. A few weeks in, I felt like I had adopted a child. She wanted to go out every night and didn't even have a job. All of a sudden, I was the way to pay her bills. When she suggested we move in together to save money, I bounced up out of there like Kangaroo Jack."

We all pretended to lick on lollipops before slowly whispering. "Sucker."

By that time Ricky had dropped the prune face and gotten into the mood. "Okay D, what's the second type."

D.C. brushed the barbeque salt off his hands. "Number two is Available Anna. She might work. She might be a student. But she is so available, that you get tired of hanging with her. She's so available that she never has plans to do anything with anybody else except you. She doesn't hang with her girls. She doesn't go out of town. She doesn't visit her people. Nothing. Bruh, that availability turns into a prison sentence for you."

I played Devil's Advocate. "But D, I thought brothers always complain about their girl not being front and center."

"True, but that's totally different. I dated this chick who was always dressed, ready to go, in my neighborhood, or something at a moment's notice. J. Edgar Hoover's surveillance on the Black Panthers probably wasn't this tight. If I called her, the phone only took half a ring before she picked up. If she called and I told her I'm hanging with y'all and won't get in until 3am she'd say, 'I'll be up. Call me.' And before you ask, I stayed with her in college because of that sweetest taboo. But when I wanted to hang with the fellas, I didn't need her blocking the exits. If I tried to dip out the side door, she'd jump in front of me to take the charge. I couldn't deal with it anymore so, when I graduated, I gave her a fake forwarding address. But I still look over my shoulder every now and then when I think about her."

Ricky clapped his hand and pointed, trying to remember. "Are you talking about Tina? D, you used to have that girl pacing back and forth between Young and Sampson Halls talking to herself."

D.C. shrugged. "Bruh, I honestly do not know how she graduated."

Luke started doing the prep. "D, you still got her number?"

D.C. chortled. "You're stupid, Luke."

Luke finished his performance off with the Reebok. "Don't get sensitive, Dawg. I'm just asking. Anyway, who's number three?"

D.C. protruded his bottom lip. "If I had to give her a name it would be Needy Nancy. You know who I'm talking about. Every day it's the same questions: 'Do you love me? Do you need me? Do you think I'm pretty?' You can't walk three steps without her latching onto your shirt like a baby kitten. The neediness will drain you. Oy, this one girl I was with used to always plead with her eyes. When I'd get up to go, she'd start that deep apologizing. 'I'm sorry. Please don't leave me. I can't make it without you.' I felt guilty for having that much power over her. Her self-esteem was so low, after a while, I didn't even want sleep with her."

I seconded that. "I feel you. That kind of woman will make you depressed just being around her. Her energy is the stickiest of the icky."

We all hee-hawed at the Dave Chappelle/Rick James reference.

D.C. followed up. "She's another one I had to give that fake address to."

We nodded in agreement and he continued. "Oh, I can't forget my girl Nagging Natasha."

Ricky smiled like he knew a few Natashas.

D.C. explained. "Natasha is the one that's always on you about something. You can't do anything right around her. All her comments boil down to hater-ade. 'You're not focused enough. You're not serious enough. You're not on your grind. You're so immature. You never take me anywhere nice.' Feel me? It's been a good minute since I've had one, but you have to watch out for 'em. They're usually the ones sitting in the middle of the club, baiting you to come and talk to her. When you finally go out and spit some game, she plays high post until you almost give up. That's how she gets control over your mind, bruh. Then, when she gives you some play, you feel so grateful that you miss what really just went down. The next thing you know, she has you in sweater vests and argyle socks."

Ricky guffawed. "I do remember seeing you looking like Boyz to Men at one of the Falcons games a few years back, but I wasn't sure it was you. Cuz, that girl from Tampa had you like that? D, that's bananas."

"I know. I'd dealt with her for three months and had had enough. She was popping that noise one day at Olive Garden so I asked her, 'If I'm such a tightwad loser with no future, why are you with me?' She claimed she never said that, but that's how she made me feel with all that sarcasm and criticism."

I shouldn't have, but I did. "D.C. I know you're not over there crying."

D.C. protested. I persisted. "Nevermind. I see you over there with the sad eyes, longing for yesterday."

Ricky butted in. "I think I've seen that look before, too."

He grinned at me. Luke shaped his mouth in an 'O' before laughing. I thought back to when I was with Giovanni. She hadn't been a nag, but I did feel sad sometimes when I thought about losing her.

I pushed back, casually. "Whatever."

Ricky prodded D.C. "So what did she say?"

"She said she only criticized me to make me better, and if I didn't want to be better then maybe we shouldn't be together."

I was back in. "Your response?"

"I paid the check, drove her home in a thunderstorm, and we haven't spoken since."

Nobody saw the weight of that one coming. Ricky broke the silence. "I hope number five is a good woman."

D.C. regrouped. "She is. I call her 'Queen to Be'."

We all broke out in a high-pitched, *Coming To America* voice. "She's Your Queen To-Ooh Beeeee..."

D.C. spoke with his hands. "That's her. See the thing about Queen is that she's beautiful, but not flawless. She's smart, but doesn't put people down about it. She's classy, but not snobby. And she's focused, man. She knows what she wants out of life and she's clear on who she is. But most of all, she's down for you. She'll tell you the truth about yourself, but it's out of love. She really does make you want to be a better man."

Ricky leaned forward. "So who is this mystery lady that got away?"

"Well, it was actually two ladies."

Luke scratched his head. D.C. elaborated. "The first time I came across a Queen was in college. She was a late bloomer and not as socially inclined as the other females on the yard. But she was funny and easy to talk to. We used to chop it up two or three times a week between classes."

Luke puzzled. "So what happened?"

"I had a certain physical type in mind and she wasn't it."

I clowned. "Was she fat?"

"Naw. When I think back on her, there is nothing I can point to that she needed to change or improve. Sure, other girls got my attention faster. But she was different. Now I know the difference is that she was a Queen. True wife material. I could be myself and she never judged me."

Luke pressed. "That still doesn't tell me what happened."

"What happened is what always happens. I met this honey-dip radiating hot tub heat and followed the flames. Queen graduated and we went our separate ways. A year later, I got a wedding invitation in the mail and felt like Vesta singing 'Congratulations'."

We all dropped our heads slightly. No one sung the chorus.

I dared. "And the second?"

"The second Queen was exactly my type. She was two years younger but we had lots in common. Things started off fast, but she was ready to go to the next level. So she borrowed a friend's apartment and made me dinner, bought me a gift, and told me how special I was to her. I told her I didn't want any titles and thought we should have an open relationship, but she was hurt and straight up vanished for a day. I finally found her sitting on the bleachers of a nearby park. She told me that we were too different, that things would never work out, and that it would hurt too much to be friends. She left town three weeks later and that was that."

I had to know. "You never looked for her?"

"Yeah, I did. I stayed up all night two years ago doing an online search for her. I saw she'd lived in Maryland and the Midwest, but the trail dead-ended at an Indiana address. The only number I could find was in her hometown and I knew she hadn't lived there since high school. But as the night went on, I got more and more desperate. So when the sun came up, I waited until about seven thirty and called the home number."

All eyes were on D.C. Through all the jokes, I never imagined the brother had that kind of perspective on things.

He leaned back and put his finger to his temple, striking the Malcolm X pose. "The phone rang twice and I wondered if it was too early to call. I planned to tell her mom I was an old friend and ask her to pass my number along. In the middle of rehearsing, she answered."

D.C. paused and swallowed.

Luke looked from side to side and tapped D.C. "Who? Her mom?"

D.C. didn't smile. "No. *She* answered."

Luke moaned. "Man, as long as we've been boys and you never told me this?"

Ricky refereed. "Let the man finish, Luke."

D.C. resumed. "I found my voice and called her name. She said 'yes' and I told her who I was. She sounded surprised so I let her know the story of my all night search."

I elbow bumped D.C. "Women love that romantic quest stuff. I'm sure she was all on you after you said that."

"Not really. She was a little short with me. I chalked it up to the last time we spoke and rolled with it. I told her I just wanted to say 'Hi' and exchange info so we could stay in contact. She hesitated, then said she didn't think her fiancé would like that."

Luke interjected. "Bombs over Bagdad."

D.C. continued. "For sure, I'm slightly stunned but thinking, if Dwayne Wayne can get Whitley, I can get my Queen."

Normally I would have dapped him up, but he still had that melancholy in his eyes.

D.C.'s chest rose and fell. "But the dagger came when she told me that the only reason she was home was to get married that weekend. I'd caught her right before breakfast with her bridesmaids."

I wished I could take back the elbow bump. She'd obviously missed that episode of *Different World*. "My bad, D."

"It's cool. I managed to get out 'I'm happy for you' and we said our goodbyes."

D.C. reached for a soda. "That's partly why I do how I do. Not sure I'll find another one. Some people are lucky to find one but I had two...and blew it."

Ricky gave me that Dr. Phil stare. "I guess losing a good woman can mess a man up for a long time, huh Timo?"

I scratched my cheek and grabbed for the remote. "I wouldn't know."

Chapter Thirty Two

Timo

Ricky called my bluff. "Oh, you're going to act all nonchalant about it?"

I pretended not to hear him. I flipped channels like that TV was the most interesting thing on earth. I drew unexpected pleasure from turning the tables on Ricky.

He persisted. "Luke, he's over here trying to play Macho Man Randy Savage."

Luke took a swipe. "Timo, a good cry never hurt anybody, dude. I heard you can lose your mind if you keep that grief pinned up inside you."

I cut my eyes at D.C., recognizing how insensitive this teasing must be given his recent confession, but kept silent and flipping.

I thought for a minute and decided to kill two birds with one stone. "You're right, Luke. Let me ask you something. You've got a shorty. I want to know if you get any flack from women about having a kid?"

Ricky started licking the inside of his mouth like a politician watching surveillance footage.

Luke's eyes registered that he understood I wasn't taking a dig at him, so he proceeded. "They ask. But when I tell them about him, it's just taken as a fact of life. Some girls think it's cute when they see me with lil' man."

D.C. came out of his daze. "That's because they don't know it's like visitation day at the County Jail for your son."

Luke fake slapped D.C. "You don't say that when you ask to borrow Eljay to walk around the Mall."

D.C. feigned offense. "Man, I paid you your money."

Ricky stopped his ears and shook his head. "That's just wrong on so many levels. Have you guys ever heard of child slavery?"

D.C. responded. "Yeah, in China. But what I do is called rent-a-kid. Man, I'm telling you, I could go on *SharkTank* and make a million."

Luke agreed. "I can't lie. It sounds messed up at first, but when you see how all kinds of women walk up to you and start conversations, you realize the kid got you to second base without even trying."

D.C. tagged in. "Single ones, married ones, kids, no kids…man you can take your pick and throw the rest back."

Ricky rubbed his eyes. "Are we really doing that bad as fathers?"

Luke fired back. "I'm a good father."

Ricky waved him off. "Not you dude, us? Are we so sad as a whole that married women will walk up to any man showing a kid some attention and throw herself at him?"

Luke smoothed down the numbers on his throwback. "What're you trying to say?"

I intervened. "He's just saying that some brothers don't like kids. Isn't that right, Rick?"

Ricky looked trapped. D.C. tried to rescue him. "Timo, you know Ricky loves the kids. He's practically running an orphanage between school and soccer practice."

By that time, Ricky and I had locked eyes, no smile. "My bad. Rick loves kids, he just doesn't think single moms are good enough to date."

"I never said that."

"Well, tell the fellas what you did say."

"I said I don't want a ready-made family and I'd prefer to date a woman with no kids."

D.C. checked the muted television. "Good luck with that."

Luke affirmed. "Man, when a woman hits her twenties, she's fertile. She's supposed to make babies. Be fruitful and multiply? Now I know that's in the Bible."

I wanted to keep my knee in Ricky's back. "Man, just because you grew up with two parents doesn't mean something is wrong with a woman because she's a single mom. You heard how D missed some good women talking that ying yang. You're about to nut up, too. No offense, D."

D.C. turned away from the pre-game festivities to inquire. "Nut up about what?"

I outted Ricky. "With Sheila."

D.C. dropped the remote, Luke bit his lip, and they both scooted their chairs closer to us.

Luke spoke with hand gestures. "You mean Sheila with that...and that?" He made a muffled screaming noise. "Man, if she wanted my attention, me and Eljay would be over there playing house right now."

D.C. came right behind. "Rick, are you telling me that you're going to let a fine creature like Sheila get away because you're hung up on her kid?"

Luke returned. "Rick she's a Trifecta: Brains, beauty, and the booty? What more could you ask for?"

Ricky shrugged.

I answered. "I'm convinced he doesn't want a good woman. He's scared of Sheila. She's smoking hot, she's smart, and she's successful."

D.C. made a declaration. "You're right Timo, he's scared."

Ricky stood up waving his shirt. "I'm not scared."

Luke covered his nose. "Rick, no need to get violent. If you're scared, say you're scared."

"I'm not scared, okay?"

I stood with him. "Then what is it?"

Rick started for the bedroom, then turned back. "I told you some of this the other day, but if it'll get you off my back, I'll tell it all."

D.C. and Luke scooted their chairs up again.

"On the real, every time I look at her shorty, it reminds me another man is in the picture that they might think is better than me—a dude that they're secretly longing for and I'm just the rebound brother putting in work somewhere that will never be my home. Man, I ain't trying to go out like that. I ain't nobody's fool."

Chapter Thirty Three

Gigi

"Counting down from 5, 4, 3, 2, 1…"

"Hi and welcome to another edition of *Atlanta Live*, Atlanta's only evening talk show that comes straight to you without edit or delay. I'm your host, Sister Vanessa, and we are blessed to be joined tonight by Giovanni George, owner of Georgian Realty and author of the upcoming book *The Love Manual*. In the last week her website, **TheLoveCommitment**.com, has had over 600,000 hits and her book already has 5,000 pre-orders. Everybody, please help me welcome Ms. Giovanni George to the show."

The studio audience clapped on cue when the blinking light flashed 'Applause'.

I clasped my hands and bowed in thanks. My leg shook whenever I had the jitters and my attempt to stop the release of adrenaline wasn't working.

But Sister Vanessa was a seasoned pro. "How're you doing tonight, Giovanni?"

"Wonderful. Thank you for having me."

"Anytime woman of God, anytime. You know how we do here on *Atlanta Live*. We're saved, but we say what needs to be said. Am I right about it?"

The audience clapped their approval.

"Now you're on *Powertalk* tomorrow morning with my friend, Lorraine Jacques White, but we've got you here first on *Atlanta Live*. So, Giovanni, tell the audience and our viewers what TLC is and why your website has experienced so many hits?"

I took a deep breath while nodding to collect my thoughts. "TLC is short for The Love Commitment and it is basically a system to help men and women who are ready and serious about family get married in two years or less."

Sister Vanessa widened her eyes and titled her head toward the audience. "Two years?"

"Or less."

"Okay. Sounds like this isn't for everybody."

"No, Sister Vanessa. This isn't for the people who are still finding themselves or couples that are casually dating without real plans for the future. This is for people who are either in a committed relationship now or people who want to be and are starting a relationship from scratch."

"And by the number of hits on your website last week alone, that must be a ton of folks."

I had a Cheshire grin. "People have responded well to The Love Commitment message."

"So your system takes people from zero to married in under two years? I gotta hear this because I'm about to shame the Devil right now. Giovanni, I hear lots of sisters around the studio talking about God being their man. I tell them, 'No, Honey. God is God. My man is my man, okay?' Just had to get that straight up in here."

The audience responded with laughter and Amen's.

Sister Vanessa followed. "In fact, I hope we can love God and love sex, too..."

She placed her hand across both her collarbones and stretched her neck. "...because it sure would be hard to give the Lord up!"

A cacophony of sniggles and 'oohs' filled the studio. Sister Vanessa leaned forward, pressing her cue cards against her chest. "Y'all can sit out there and look deep if you want to. Paul said it's better to marry than to burn. Girl, burning is not my gift."

The laughter continued and I noticed that my leg had stopped shaking. Sister Vanessa raised her cheekbones and segued back to me. "Giovanni, they're out there playing. I'm not. So tell us how to get this man to the altar in record time."

I unclasped my hands. "The first thing is truly getting to know yourself: your wants, your needs, your likes, and your dislikes. If you know yourself, you know the kind of man you want and need. The big secret is that we thought we were looking for the right man. Really, we needed to spend that time getting connected with ourselves. Most importantly, before dealing with TLC, a woman has to be able to answer these two questions: (1) What are my goals and (2) What are my personal values? The data shows that people with similar goals and values not only get married to each other, but are more likely to stay married and have happier marriages."

"So should I carry the psychological evaluations around with me? Because you know I can get the big purse."

The laughter light flashed above our heads.

"No need. In Phase I, all it takes are a few easy questions to get things started."

"I see you like those questions. But before you get into them, is this system only for women or can men use it, too?"

"As you can guess, given the biological clock, it's primarily female driven; but men who are ready to be married cannot only use this system, but will probably have better results."

Sister Vanessa fanned with her cards and motioned for me to dish up the goods.

"Phase I is called 'The Weed Out' and the questions are open-ended. It consists of three dates, at least a week apart, and each date focuses on a specific question. You will, of course, small talk for a time, but the main event of these Phase I dates are 'The Weed Out' questions. Question #1 is: 'Tell me everything that comes to mind about yourself.' Now as women, we have a tendency to be chatty and spill our story, but never get his. This is the time you use that poise you learned at church, cross your legs, and just listen."

"What if he starts asking you about yourself?"

"You can tell him...after you get enough information to make a decision about whether the next date is necessary. Make a game of it. If he likes you he'll play along. If not, you might have your answer from that."

Sister Vanessa scratched at her index cards. "You see me over here taking notes? Keep going."

"If you like what you hear and no red flags pop up, then you can safely move on to Date and Question #2."

Sister Vanessa stretched out her hand. "If I understand you correctly, the first date is for background data?"

"Correct. This is crucial because you want to know if he has a good relationship with his family, is a loner, has kids, has been married, is employed, is fresh out of a long-term relationship, etc... Without this intel, you're flying blind into parts unknown."

"Amen to that. Tell me more."

"Question #2 is: 'What are your goals?' Say nothing after asking this question; just wait. If he asks whether you mean short term or long term, tell him both."

Sister Vanessa adjusted her sitting position. "So what are you looking for him to say?"

"Nothing in particular. But whatever his goals are, they need to match up with yours. In other words, you need to be able to see how your goals connect with his."

"Can you give us an example of connecting goals?"

"Sure. Let's say one of his goals is to own a restaurant. My best friend and co-founder of thelovecommitment.com always says, without a written plan, a goal is no more than a wish."

Sister Vanessa gave an emphatic nod.

I returned the gesture. "So on Date #2, you need to find out if he has a written plan to achieve his goals."

"If he doesn't, is it a deal-breaker?"

"Not necessarily. But it shows you what level he's on. It shows how much thought and preparation he puts and will put into things, including you. If his goals match yours, you can always help him commit a plan to paper."

"What if you don't have a written plan for your own goals?"

"Then you need to get one before asking a man about his."

Sister Vanessa turned to the audience. "You hear that women of God? Write your plan first. So much revelation in that one statement."

A few audience members pulled pens from their purses. I resumed. "But if things don't match up, do not force them. If you have a written plan to pay off your mortgage, quit your job, and become a missionary, you won't be much help to him in the restaurant business and there's not much help he can give you either. You have two different life paths. Accept this fact, be grown about it, and don't waste his time or your own."

I paused for dramatic effect. "We women are notorious time-wasters when it comes to romance. Just like in real estate, money is made when you buy, not when you sell. The same is true in relationships: marriages are made when you meet, not when you mate."

"I like that, girl. Say it with me ladies: 'Marriages are made when you meet, not when you mate.' I'm definitely stealing that one."

I let that mantra soak in and continued. "Sister Vanessa, I've wasted so much time on men that never shared my goals, and then blamed them for wasting my time. I had to face the fact that the only person who can waste my time is me."

Sister Vanessa kicked up her right leg. "Girl, you're going to start a revival in here. Watch it!"

She waved her right hand, closed it into a fist, and jerked her body. "Let me go ahead and confess that you cut me deep with that time-wasting remark. I'm the chief sinner on that one."

The audience giggled and Sister Vanessa flipped her note card. "Giovanni, hurry up and tell us the third question so we can figure out if this is the right man for us."

The female audience members gave a thunderous applause without the light flashing. "Okay ladies, you've spent the past couple of weeks thinking over who this man says he is, what he says his goals are, and asking yourself if these answers match your own. If he has survived the first two dates, he obviously has your interest. This is the last 'Weed Out Date' so the question tonight has two parts. The first is: 'What things do you value most in life and why?' The second is: 'Where do you see yourself in the next two years?' Again, say nothing after asking these questions. Pay attention to both *what* he says and *how* he says it. Your future depends on it. "

"Are you looking for any particular answers at this point?"

"Yes ma'am. This is not his life story or interests. The first question is about his motivations, the second question is about his intentions. Without prompting, he needs to tell you that one of his highest values is family and that in the next two years he sees himself in a committed relationship. He may not say those exact words, but if he doesn't emphatically tell you this, he's not in the same place you are and you have a decision to make."

"Which is?"

"You can continue to see him and give the relationship an artificial boost by overlooking those red flags, or you can tell him that you're looking for something more substantial, part as friends, and meet someone else."

Sister Vanessa looked from side to side, breathless. "Wow. You're no nonsense when it comes to men. I'm scared of you."

The audience agreed and she continued. "Giovanni, you have a successful real estate company and you're a beautiful woman. Why did you create the website and write the book?"

The last five years flashed before my eyes. "Sister Vanessa, I dated a man for three years that I wanted to marry. We lived together, slept together, the whole nine. But he told me all along that he didn't want to get married. Instead of listening to him and the red flags, I drowned them out with my desires and things ended in disaster. It was obvious from the beginning that he wasn't for me, but I had to face the fact that I really played myself."

Sister Vanessa handed me some tissue. "But it's funny you mentioned my company because I came across some information while doing business that completely opened my mind to what it means to make a love commitment. Trust me, it's not what we've been doing and women back in the day got married at much higher rates because they had a system in place that everybody accepted. Once my friend Sheila and I figured this out, we understood that the only way to help ourselves form a love commitment is to help other women form love commitments as well."

"So this isn't simply altruistic?"

"Oh, no. Can I be real with you?"

"Please do."

"Sister Vanessa, we are truly our sister's keeper but, just like real estate, this is business all the way around. Sisters have got to handle their business on all levels. Love commitments are no different. For me to get mine, I have to help you get yours."

"On that note, we'll find out exactly when a love commitment occurs after our commercial break. Don't you touch that dial. We'll be right back."

Chapter Thirty Four

Timo

All eight eyes were glued to the set. I stroked the hair between my bottom lip and chin. Luke clapped his hands. "Timo, I don't know how you're alive with those tread marks on your back. Dude, Giovanni threw you up under the bus."

D.C. was next. "Oy, usually I don't kick a man when he's down, but there's no need. Giovanni already stomped you into wine."

Ricky completed the triangle. "At least she didn't say your name, bruh."

I couldn't hold it any longer. "At least? Between Google and the social networks, everybody and their grandma will know I'm the guy she's talking about in thirty minutes."

Luke grinned with his mouth open. "At least you'll be famous."

I snapped back. "Dude, I don't need this kind of drama when my business is just getting off the ground. My players are in contract negotiations and when they come out with the money, they'll expect me to be stable. If I'm in the tabloids or on Jerry Springer, how stable will I look? This could ruin everything."

D.C. offered his two cents. "Calm down fake Dean Witter. Nobody will be Googling you. From where I sit, everybody will be hitting **T**he**L**ove**C**ommitment.com to get the scoop on Giovanni's system. So don't worry, you're still Mr. Invisible."

I made a punching gesture at D.C., but his words did console me in an offhanded way. What I need to do is beat Giovanni at her own game by mastering that system. But how?

Chapter Thirty Five

Gigi

"And welcome back to *Atlanta Live*. For those who are just tuning in, our special guest is Ms. Giovanni George—co-founder of **T**he**L**ove**C**ommitment.com and author of the forthcoming book, *The Love Manual*. Giovanni, before the break, you were telling us about a love commitment being business and I think we all know that by how you broke down those initial questions. But do we have a love commitment if we get through the first three dates?"

I held up my index finger before responding. "A love commitment is like a house. You've got to take your time pouring the foundation. When that is solid, then you can pick up the pace. After the first three dates, the 'Weed Out' Phase is complete. Now you're in what we call a 'Decision Moment'. These Decision Moments arise at the end of every phase and they're where you have to be a big girl and either decide to halt the proceedings in the current phase or move forward to the next phase."

"I see. So what's the next phase?"

"If you decide to move forward, the next date is what we call 'An Offer Date'. I know it sounds like a lot, but so did driving a car until you got the hang of it. Stay with me and I promise it'll all make sense."

Sister Vanessa turned to the audience. "I'm good. Are you all good?" The audience roared. "Yes!"

She patted my knee. "Go ahead and teach, girl."

"Great. The offer goes something like this: 'From what I know of you, you're the kind of man I've been looking for. If you feel the same about me, can we agree to spend the next couple of months figuring out if this is infatuation or the real thing? The only thing I ask is that we're totally honest with each other."

I let out a huff of air. "Now here is a critical piece of the system. During this time kissing and hugging are fine, but no sex."

Sister Vanessa made a zero with her hand. "None?"

"None."

"Nada?"

"Nada."

"I guess the Word does say that. Well do you have to be strong in your faith to do this?" Sister Vanessa waved her hand. "See if I talk about them they'll get mad, so I'll talk about me. Sometimes a sister gets a little weak."

I rocked and laughed.

Sister Vanessa faux frowned. "You said 'be honest', right? I'm just being honest."

"No, I perfectly understand. And, to your point, you may have to quote some Scripture to keep your resolve. But the success of this system does not depend on your religion. It really depends on you knowing yourself, staying focused, and women sticking together."

"What do you mean?"

"I mean besides all the women who never get married or end up being single moms, over half the women that do get married end up getting divorced. Don't you think those divorced women would say it would have been worth it to slow down and take sex out of the picture to keep things clear?"

"I imagine so. But if we're going to keep it one hundred, women like sex and have sexual needs, too. It's not just men."

This time I patted her knee. "Don't I know it? But what I didn't know is that when two people have sex, there is a hormone called oxytocin that is released during orgasm. When this happens, an emotional bond begins to form and, the more sex they have, the stronger the bond gets. The problem comes in if you are chemically bonding when you need to be thinking and observing. And guess who releases more oxytocin?"

The audience screamed. "Women!"

"You guessed it. Estrogen magnifies the effect of oxytocin; which is why we fall in love harder and faster, even if we know the man is not compatible with us. That's when we start trying to change men. And that never works."

"You sat right on my pew with that one, Giovanni."

"It's my pew, too. The good news is lower doses of oxytocin are released through hugging and touch, so you can still bond and keep a level head at the same time."

Sister Vanessa had a twinkle in her eye. "Okay, since you said you don't have to be religious for the system to work, when does the system say you *can* have sex?"

"Given the growing statistics about single moms, I recommend no sex until marriage. But, for people who think this is impossible, sex should at least be off the table until a love commitment has been established."

"I think I speak for everybody when I ask this next question: 'When is a love commitment established?"

"A love commitment happens with a public engagement to be married."

"So you're saying no sex until you put a ring on it?"

"Yes. And I'm also saying the moment of proposal isn't necessarily the moment of love commitment. A Love Commitment requires a public declaration of intention, like an engagement party, large dinner, or at least a cookout. It should be some event where the couple announces to the world that they are moving toward marriage in good faith."

"But in the company of witnesses?"

"The more the merrier."

"Giovanni, this may be on many women's mind, but will ladies be seen as pushy if they present the love commitment instead of men?"

"They could be. Women are socialized to let and look for men to drive the courting process. That used to be cool in the distant past but, with our modern outlook, that's fantasy for many of us. For a long time I only blamed men for dodging commitment, lying, or cheating, but I had to accept that the key to solving the marriage problem is within us."

"Women?"

"Women sticking together in unity."

"How so?"

"Sis, men refuse to commit mainly because they don't have to. They can go anywhere in the city and have ten women. In a city like Atlanta with six million people, you could never know everybody. But if women learn to think alike when it comes to relationships and commitment, we could change the world in favor of marriage, families, and our children."

"Giovanni, let me play Devil's Advocate for a minute. What about the guy who commits to you but is sex-starved and gets a little on the side? If he said, 'The Love Commitment structure caused me to cheat', what would you say?"

"If that happened I'd say the system worked perfectly."

"Huh?"

"The timeframe between meeting and marriage is up to the individual couple. If the guy is not ready to be in that kind of relationship, he is always free to let the woman know and walk away. We may not like it, but we will respect it. However, if he stays *and* cheats, then he's not the guy you need at that time and the system showed that."

"Child, you said a mouthful then. Listen, we're almost out of time but I have to ask you: Is it realistic to think that women will stick together on this? The sister he cheated with obviously wasn't on the same page, so is it reasonable to think that enough women would unify to make this work?"

I felt a perspiration drop slide down my ribcage. "It's funny you ask because we just had a focus group where that was the main concern. To be frank, there will always be skeezers who disrespect your relationship and there will always be lying men who don't tell women that they are involved with someone else. That's life. But this is why shows like yours are so important. We have to make sure that every woman, everywhere goes to **TheLoveCommitment**.com and orders a copy of *The Love Manual*. We have to form book clubs, reading circles, and support groups to reinforce these concepts. This system has to become second nature to all women. We have to teach it to our daughters and we also have to teach it to our sons. When this happens, our women and our men will pattern their relationships after a love commitment that is family-centered. There will still be people who do their own thing, but they'll become the exception again and folks in love commitments will be the norm."

"Before I let you go, I'm sure we're all dying to know if you have a love commitment of your own and, if so, his name please?"

My face flushed. "No names, but I am in negotiations with a promising candidate. So let's just say that I'm working on it."

The applause light flashed overhead. Sister Vanessa's voice was upbeat. "And there you have it. Our guest today has been Ms. Giovanni George, owner of Georgian Realty and author of *The Love Manual* scheduled to be released one month from today. You can get it online or anywhere books are sold. As a matter of fact, buy ten copies and give one to every woman in your circle. You can also order the book through her website, thelovecommitment.com, where she explains what she told us today, but the book goes into much greater detail. From the way the switchboard is lighting up backstage, we may need to have her back soon after the book's release. Until then, thank you for tuning in. I'm your host, Sister Vanessa, and we'll see you tomorrow on the next edition of *Atlanta Live*. Goodnight."

Chapter Thirty Six

Timo

I shot out of there faster than Don King being chased by a mob with a straightening comb. The crew laughed about me needing some fresh air as I closed the door. They might've laughed harder if I'd told them exactly where I was going. So I didn't mention it. They'd press me and I'd explain later. Right then, my mind was single: lay back on the steps and wait.

After the engine shut off, the alarm chirped shortly before she did. "What are you doing here?"

"I came by to congratulate you on the interview."

Giovanni sauntered past me swinging her keys. "Oh, you saw it?"

"Yeah, I saw it. And I wanted to set a few things straight."

"Timo, I can't talk right now. I need to freshen up for my date."

"With who?"

"Wouldn't you like to know?"

"I would."

"Timo, I don't have time for this. I need to get ready."

Giovanni turned the key. I followed close behind to avoid being left outside.

She tossed her key ring into a wicker basket on the counter and headed to the back bedroom. "I thought you already pumped Sheila on the details of my private life."

I sat on the living room sofa and spread my arms across the top. "She told me a few things about you hitting the skids hard on the rebound. I'm here to make things better for you."

Giovanni peeked around the dividing wall. "Whatever Timo. For your information, Eric is a caring and lovely man who is focused and wants what I want out of life. Not at all like you. So if you will excuse me, I'm going to shower before he gets here. Since you let yourself in, I'm sure you can let yourself out."

Giovanni ducked back behind the wall ten seconds before shower water began to flow.

I shouted. "You know, if you needed a date that bad, I could've fixed you up with some better choices than the Geek Squad."

She didn't respond so I picked up the *Essence Magazine* on her coffee table. I didn't get past the cover taglines before the doorbell rang.

I mouthed at a volume less than a shout. "I'll get it."

The man that stood before me was about my height, wore a charcoal grey suit with a light peach oxford, no tie. His stylish spectacles accented the knit of his eyebrows while he deciphered the reason for my presence.

I extended my hand. "You must be Eric. I'm Timo. Giovanni's in the shower but she should be out any minute. Can I get you something to drink?"

Eric warily crossed the threshold and mirrored my steps as I backpedaled. "Thank you, no."

"You sure? We have cold juice and soda."

Eric's expression turned from confusion to bewilderment. He looked as if he could use a Captain Midnight Secret Decoder Ring right about now. "Who are you, again?"

The abrupt halting of water froze his question in midair. Giovanni's footsteps could be heard moving toward us along with her words. "I hope you're not still here. I told you I..."

Giovanni appeared from the hallway wrapped in a towel, shoulders wet and exposed. She screamed and crossed her arms to cover. "Eric?"

Like a mouthful of Milk Duds, she took us both in at the same time. "What are you doing here?"

I looked to Eric for an explanation. His jacket rose along with his hands. "What?"

Giovanni retorted. "Not you. You?"

Their eyes hit me from both directions. I packed as much disbelief into my response as I could muster. "Who me?"

Giovanni snapped back. "Timo, you need to leave. I told you I was going out."

Both Eric and I stood mesmerized by Giovanni's moist skin and walnut eyes. I sensed Eric's arousal as she stomped down the corridor to get dressed. And by the clenched teeth I saw when I turned back toward him, he sensed mine."

I acted quickly. "Uh, Giovanni told me you're a professor at Emory. How do you like it?"

The transition of conversation to his terrain made him relax a hair. "It's a good school. And you?"

This was the measuring game boys played with each other. No matter how old we got, it all boiled down to a peeing contest. "I'm at Merrill, for now. Doing my own thing, too. Nobody's going to give you what belongs to you. You've got to take it."

Previous tension re-established. "So Eric, how do you know Giovanni again?"

He opened and closed his fingers. "I was the first man she met in Atlanta."

"Really? That's funny. She never mentioned you to me before tonight."

He scoffed. "And how do you know her."

"Oh, we go way back." I rocked on my heels, feigning to lose my balance. "Way back."

I smiled and pinch-rubbed my nose. Before he could respond, Giovanni reappeared in a black, form-fitting dress that accentuated her best features and tapered mid-thigh. She knew that was my favorite.

"Yes, Timo is an old, old friend who was just leaving."

Giovanni grabbed my elbow and put her other hand in the small of my back, pushing me toward the door.

"This feels familiar."

Giovanni tightened her grip on my elbow and picked up the pace.

"Oh, you're just going to...? It's like that?"

I thought better of it with Stephen Hawking watching and composed myself. "That's cool."

When we got to the door, Giovanni opened it. I braced myself on the doorframe and swiveled my head. "I'm sure I'll see you again, bruh."

I turned back and looked down at Giovanni. "Later Babes."

She nudged me out onto the front porch with a muffled slam.

I massaged my left buttock from the doorknob indentation and shouted at the door. "Dawg! It's not like I've never seen you naked before."

Through my scowl, I noticed a dark brown mass moving from the periphery of my right eye. It spoke. "Sorry sir. Didn't mean to startle you. Mr. George?"

He handed me a clipboard to sign and then a package addressed to Giovanni.

"Sir, for what it's worth, my wife puts me out once a week. I just take a drive to clear my head and, when I come back, we're both as good as new."

The UPS guy started down the walkway. I almost left the package on the banister and went with him. But then a thought crossed my mind after giving the box a shake. I flipped open the lid, surveyed the contents, and danced all the way to my car.

Chapter Thirty Seven

Gigi

I prolonged my stare at the door, avoiding turning around as long as I could. "Eric I'm so sorry about that. He was on my steps when I got home from the taping."

"Ex-boyfriend?"

I met Eric's eyes. "Quadruple-X. I haven't seen him in three years until the other night and now he's popping up all over the place."

"Is he stalking you?"

"No, nothing like that. This was the only time I think he tried to see me. The other night was a chance encounter."

"I get it. Well, he did seem to know his way around your space."

I flattened my lips. "Typical Timo. We lived together in an apartment for a year and a half so he knows how I live. With him, it's always a childish attempt to assert dominance."

Eric nodded. "I have to admit it was pretty effective. I was off-balance for a minute there."

I sashayed closer. "So what can I do to make it up to you?"

Eric smiled. "No need. In fact, I can't blame a man for trying."

He titled his head to the left. "Now you're sure there's nothing between you two?"

I laced my arms around his neck. "That's been over for years. Besides, he's not half the man you are."

With that, I gave Eric a sample of my lip gloss and he led me to dinner.

Timo

I walked in whistling a tune I'd just heard on the radio. The toilet flushed and Ricky appeared.

"Where'd you go?"

"I ran an errand and hit Indie."

Indie Coffee and Books was where Ricky and I went to hang and veg. No talking, just coffee and reading until our eyeballs hurt.

"Without me?"

"My bad. I had to take care of something first."

"I'll bet. The way you bolted outta here, we thought you ran out of hemorrhoid cream."

"Funny. But I only had a few minutes to get there."

Ricky smirked and motioned to my package. So what was so important that you had to run out in traffic barefoot?"

"Nunya."

"If it's in my crib, it's my business. Especially when it says Giovanni George on the address label."

Ricky had better than 20/20 vision. He could read road signs that were mere blips in the distance to the rest of us. I tossed it over. "See for yourself."

Ricky dumped the contents onto the table. "*The Love Manual*? Why does it look like a photocopy?"

"It's the galley that the publisher sends out for corrections or for critics to get a sneak peek."

"So how did you get it?"

"I have my ways."

"You know that mail theft is a crime, right?"

"Hey, it was handed to me and I signed for it so, technically, I didn't steal it."

"Tell it to the judge."

"You can't spoil my victory tonight, Ricky. In fact, you should be happy."

"Why's that?"

"Because I'm giving you a chance to peep the system." I reached for the book. "Unless you don't want to know how Sheila's thinking?"

Ricky snatched the box before I could get to it.

I smiled. "Thought so."

Ricky thumbed through the manuscript. "During the interview, Giovanni said that a love commitment happens with a public engagement, but she didn't tell us the steps between Weed Out and Love Commitment."

Ricky flipped back to the table of contents. I put him out of his misery. "That would be Phase 2 and Phase 3: Verification and Exclusive."

Ricky's index finger stopped sliding. "I see you actually did read at Indie. Well, spill it."

I sat back and crossed my legs like Tony Sinclair on the Tanqueray commercial, sporting a British accent. "Ricky my good man, we mustn't rush such delectable delicacies."

Ricky resumed his finger slide and rifled through the pages. "Uh, it says here that the Verification Phase is when the couple discovers (1) if what the other has said about him/herself is true, (2) if the other is really the person you want, (3) if you are truly ready to form a love commitment, and (4) if you are ready to form a love commitment with this person."

I uncrossed my legs. "Yeah, I read all that. Sounded like a whole lot of double checking to me."

"You'd better double check if you only plan to get married once."

"I guess. But what are you supposed to do to verify what a person says?"

"Giovanni says be observant. All you're doing is weighing their actions against their words to see if they match up."

"Rick, everybody's got a little hypocrite in them. The fitness guru who gorges on sweet potato pie. The financial expert whose credit cards are maxed out. If we dig deep enough, we all wear the mask that grins and lies."

"Thank you, Paul Laurence Dunbar. But she seems to be referring to blatant contradictions between your story and your life, not your points of improvement."

"No. Thank *you*, Bertice Berry, for explaining the female point of view."

"Whatever dude. Anyway, what's the Exclusive Phase?"

"The phase she was trying to start with that dude who ditched her at *Justin's*."

"Right. Exclusive dating with the intention of moving toward marriage. I remember that. But how long between that and the love commitment?"

"I think the book says up to three months for the one year plan, six months for the eighteen month plan, and nine months for the two year plan."

Ricky filled his jaws with air. "So from 'Day 1' to engagement can be six, nine, or twelve months depending on the plan you follow?"

"Pretty much."

Ricky thought it over and asked another question while he still had Timo's attention. "I get that the system says ideally no sex until marriage and that some folks will choose to have sex after the engagement, so how much time does the system have between engagement and marriage?"

I put my feet on the table. "You sure are asking a lot of questions."

"Do you know the answer?"

"Yeah. You should, too."

"Huh?"

"If you're on the one year plan, engagement is six months. For the eighteen month plan, engagement is nine months. And for the two year plan, engagement is twelve months. The manual says if you can't see yourself married in two years or less, you're probably not ready to commit."

"I told you Timo, that's dog years to a woman."

"According to the way Giovanni wants it done, they are dry years if you know what I mean."

Ricky stood, shaking the manual at me. "You know Timo, you should go ahead and confess your love for Giovanni and get it over with."

I closed my eyes and rested my head on the chair top. "You must not be taking your medicine."

Ricky lifted his chin. "What else explains you hiding in her bushes and commandeering her mail?"

"She'll never miss it."

"I doubt that, but I like how you avoided the issue."

I did dance down the sideline like Walter Payton, but I'd never tell Ricky. "Bruh, I've got her whole system and she doesn't even know it." I went into my Black Belt Theater accent. "Sun Tsu say each battle won before first shot fired."

"What?"

I enlightened my compatriot. "You win by having tactical advantage. Positioning is power. And if you know where to stand, your opponent, no matter how strong, can never defeat you."

Ricky held up the manual. "Alright, Blackie Chan. So I take it you're not giving this back?"

"No sireee bob."

"In that case, you won't mind me skimming it before I go to bed."

Like a cat, Ricky darted for his room. I reached his door just in time to hear the lock click and deadbolt fasten.

Chapter Thirty Eight

Gigi

I was hanging up the phone when Sheila walked in.

"G, who was that?"

"Mr. George."

"From down the street?"

"Yep."

"You two-timing Eric for an 80 year old?"

"Nope."

"So what's up?"

"Something I can't quite put my finger on yet."

Sheila zipped her purse, tossed it, took a seat, and listened.

"I was on the phone with my editor earlier. He called to ask how I liked the book layout, but I told him I hadn't received it yet. Funny thing is, he said he checked an email this morning with a picture of the delivery confirmation receipt."

Sheila's brow furrowed.

"He read it to me and the signature just said 'George'."

"When was it delivered?"

"The time stamp says last night around the time I left with Eric. I called Mr. George down the street to find out if UPS delivered it to him by accident, but he said it didn't come to him. And if it had, he would have signed his full name: George Henry Speights."

"So where could it be?"

"I'm still thinking. Meanwhile, the editor sent another one overnight to the UPS store. I can pick it up from there after 8am tomorrow."

"I can't wait to see it."

"Me either. And neither can Mr. George. He wouldn't let me get off the phone unless I promised to autograph three copies for him. He insisted that he pay for them."

"How does he even know what it's about?"

"Girl, he saw the interview yesterday. It's a trip. He said in his day, men used to court women the way I described, but now courting has been replaced with macking. He wants to keep a copy for himself and give one to his granddaughter and his grandson."

"Gigi, you were a monster on that interview. You killed it."

"Thanks to you, Sheila. You're the one that hooked it up."

"I'm telling you G, all I did was mention the concept in my single's ministry group and one of the sisters knew Vanessa. So don't thank me, thank God."

"I have. Sister Vanessa said they got three hundred calls that day requesting DVDs of the show."

"And the site hits spiked 50,000 during the broadcast. Gigi, promoting marriage and family is right and I believe that God blesses things that bless others."

"Sheila, to be honest, I didn't expect things to get so big so fast. I haven't had much time to focus on my business."

"G, your biggest piece of business is Storie's house and, like you said, it'll sell itself."

"Yeah, I know. I just never planned on becoming Dr. Phil. I'm having a PR crisis here. Not that I'm complaining, but I guess the love commitment has shifted some things around."

"Speaking of love commitments, what's up with Eric?"

I clasped my hands like Julie Andrews in *The Sound of Music*. "He's wonderful. We had dinner last night at Crawfish Shack."

"In Druid Hills?"

"Yeah girl, you know I like it spicy."

"I see. Well, I hope you kept your pants on."

I let out a high, staccato yelp. "Sheila, you don't have to worry about me. You're the one I'm worried about. I expect to read about you streaking butt naked across the soccer field one day jumping on Ricky."

"I wish."

"What?"

"I mean, 'you wish'."

Sheila laughed and let out a long 'whooooo' afterward. "Girl, I haven't spoken to Ricky since that time at the library. And Diamond hasn't mentioned him, either."

"That doesn't mean you haven't been thinking about him. I'll bet you're sleeping with a pillow between your knees."

Sheila was slow to answer. "That was probably just a one day spark."

I had noted Sheila's attempts at modesty and understatement all afternoon. "If it were, you wouldn't be looking like a hound dog with sagging jowls and big floppy ears."

"Is it that obvious?"

"Yes, but it's a cute contrast from your usual gunslinger persona. And from what I hear, Ricky is a brainiac like you. Two peas in a pod. Or should I say two brains in a jar?"

That got Sheila to show some teeth. Right before she wiped two tears away.

"What's wrong?"

"Girl, I was over here fantasizing about God sending me a good man and a father for Diamond. I just got full. I'll be alright."

"I did hear Rev say you have not because you ask not."

Sheila pursed her lips. "Child, it's not because I haven't been asking. But some things are about timing and preparation. Either way, all I can do is concentrate on being a good mother and businesswoman until God moves."

"Sheila, I hate to sound heathenistic, but I disagree completely.

Girl, this is exactly why we created the site. It's why you encouraged me to write the book. And it's why we found that chest with the Black Victorian pamphlet. It's all been moving us in this direction."

"What direction?"

"To form love commitments of our own and model them for everyone to see. That's how people will know it works."

Sheila brushed her shoes across the carpet a time or two. I continued. "But it's not just for them. First and foremost it's for you and me. We deserve to be happy and why should we wait for a guy to see skywriting, fifty-four sermons, and forty-three prophecies before he decides to maybe see if something might kind of happen between us? I believe that when a man finds a wife he finds a good thing, but I also believe that when a woman knows how to present herself to a man, it's much easier for him to find her."

Sheila pulled a citrus wine cooler from her purse and lifted it in the air. "I'll drink to that."

Before I could relax my expression she rejoined. "A little wine for my stomach, Gigi. Mommy's got to get loose sometimes; especially when you're saying I need to work my mojo."

I leaned forward. "I'm glad you're feeling so cozy. Now here's what we're going to do."

Chapter Thirty Nine

Timo

I'd hoped against it, but the NFL Owners and the Players' Union didn't come to terms as of midnight last night. The players threatened to strike but, believe it or not, most of them live paycheck to paycheck; in spite of how lavish and luxurious their lifestyles appear to be. League minimum is $250,000 a year. But when Uncle Sam gets through with them, 33% of that is gone, leaving less than $170,000. After the agent, the private trainer, the house, the cars, the wife, the kids, the bills, the baby mama, and the ever present donation basket get a hold of that 170, it can start to look like minimum wage. I forgot to mention all the friends, relatives, and long, lost cousins that try to make you remember how close you used to be before you got drafted.

In that mixed bag of company, there's only one unmentioned person among them who's worth his weight in gold. And that would be me: the financial planner. I'm the guy in the equation that keeps the money growing so that there's lots of it to live on after the 'Big Give' is done. I invest in stocks, bonds, acquire businesses, set up non-profits, I do it all. I complete all the tax returns for my players and, for some, I write the checks, lick the envelopes, and pay their bills every month...for a small fee, of course. All of this came to a grinding halt while I slept last night.

The owners are pushing to keep more revenue from gross sales so they initiated a lockout where the players are forbidden to work until the two sides come to an agreement. I have some cash saved because of my living situation, but chomping through my money sock is not a good thing for a person in my line of business. My two biggest clients ever are hanging in limbo and their pending contracts will be advertisement for securing future signees. There's a lot riding on this for me so, after I called my players and their parents, I took a drive to unwind, bumping my boy Phil Collins.

At Merrill what I do is client-based so, until the lockout is over, I had some time on my hands. I decided to be productive and sit in on a class to brush up on my African American Studies.

The Candler Library towered on the quaint campus and housed several smaller auditoriums seating at least two hundred people each. I stepped into the aisle of the two-story Reading Room which, from the looks of the overhead pedestrian bridge, had been both restored and renovated. Finally reaching the classroom corridor, I broke the seal of the door and witnessed most students listening to the lecture, watching the PowerPoint, or taking copious notes. Some were catching up on much needed or much desired sleep. I slipped into the napping section through the side door and slumped down with my cap pulled over my forehead.

"To whom is Carter G. Woodson referring with the label 'Mis-educated Negro?"

A few hands went up in the front. "Yes, Mr. Johnson?"

"He meant black people that went to school but never learned to read or write."

Eric placed the remote control to his lips. "Perhaps. Ms. Lewis?"

"He meant bourgeois black folks who think because they go to college they're better than black people who don't."

He lowered the controller to his tie. "Hmmm. Interesting. Anyone else?"

For a beat, no one raised their hand. Then an upward motion brushed against my sleeve. I slid to the right and swiveled left. A scruffy young man with an oversized Marcus Garvey t-shirt, cornrows, and a pair of green G-Nikes held his hand suspended above.

Eric lifted his chin. "In the back?"

My neighbor stood. "Dr. Haynes, on a surface level, Woodson refers to some of the persons my classmates mentioned as mis-educated. But his real targets are African Americans who attend the University and are taught to despise and undermine all things black and African. These individuals become professionals, K-12 teachers, and even college professors who live or teach in a way that conveys Europe as the paragon of culture and progress, while dismissing the African Diaspora as primitive and backwards."

"Well said Mr..."

"Rivers. Pearl Rivers."

"Mr. Rivers, do you have anything else to offer?"

"Just that if Woodson were alive today, he might also add all African American college students to the list of mis-educated negroes for borrowing $150,000 to get degrees that teach us very few tangible skills and only bring us $40,000 paychecks."

Eric crossed his arms. "What would you say if I told you that we don't teach skills here, we teach you to think critically. And if you want job training, you need to enroll at a vocational or technical school?"

The male Pearl crossed his arms in return. "No disrespect. But I'd ask you if the kids borrowing $150,000 to go here *know* that you're not training them to get a job?"

All the sleepers were wide awake. Eric uncrossed his arms and replaced his thumb on the remote. "None taken."

He turned back to the screen. "Next class we'll look at the Booker T. Washington/W.E.B. Dubois debate on educational philosophy as well as their differing views of African American progress. Be sure to read Chapter 6 and keep in mind that we're in a summer session so the pace is accelerated. See you tomorrow."

The class filed out in all directions. I leapt into the flow of traffic and blended like a disoriented movie-goer being swept toward the exit by a throng of chatty teenagers. I bustled along but perched my left eye on Eric as he packed his satchel. Two female students asked him questions. He answered without looking up.

I didn't have anything against Eric. I just needed to understand my competition. If I had been speaking aloud I would've said 'the professor' or 'Mr. Rebound', but the scolding I gave myself for being honest reflected the truth. Eric was my competition and he had something I didn't have. A clean record with Giovanni. Anything I could find out would strengthen my quest. Not that I would outright snitch on Eric's misdeeds if uncovered. That would betray the man-code and undermine my own self-respect. But I would conveniently leak the information employing other channels and assets. As a general rule, men don't blatantly squeal on other men to secure female affection. The two exceptions are if the woman receiving the information is a relative or platonic friend. Otherwise, it's a punk move. At that moment, my state of mind was best described as in control, but leaning toward rule-bending.

I tailed Eric to his office and watched a few students go in and out, mostly women. A line of six or seven stood against his outer wall, anticipating a conversation before the conference hour ended. One student meeting had lasted nearly thirty minutes and the others murmured among themselves about the time being hogged. When she emerged from the closed door session, I met her at the elevator. My pleasant energies were channeled from a place deep inside.

"Hi. I'm Tim."

She pressed the down button. "Candace."

"Hi Candace. I saw you in that last class."

"You're a student here?"

"Not yet. But I'll be a grad student in the fall, so I dropped by to get a feel for the place and sit in on a few classes. What year are you?"

"Senior, but I'll be a grad student here in the fall, too."

Candace faced me squarely. "What's your area?"

"My background is finance and I'm drawn to Diasporic fiscal policy and practices." I'd picked that word up from Pearl.

Her eagerness helped her to disregard my clumsiness with the term. "Then you may want to start with a domestic revisitation of places like Idlewild & Black Wall Street prior to shifting into the currents of the International Monetary Fund and how it has ravaged the economies and exports of our sister nations in Haiti and Jamaica."

I was genuinely impressed. Perhaps because I understood most of what she'd said. "Wow. You've got your history and economics on lock. Have you picked a major professor yet?"

"Dr. Haynes, all the way."

"That brother who taught the seminar? He did seem pretty cool in class. If you're not busy, I'd love to hear about his specialty and the Department in general."

Her eyes brightened. "Sure. I'm headed over to the Union. You're welcome to come. We can talk there if you don't mind."

That'll be perfect. I don't know where the Union is so it'll be like a talk and a tour rolled up into one. It was just my luck running into you."

The down button light went out and the elevator doors opened wide. I bowed slightly. "After you."

Chapter Forty

Timo

I-85 North is nothing nice when you're fighting traffic at rush hour. In Atlanta, rush hour can last from 3-8pm if you get stuck on the wrong freeway. I bought Candace a soda and she educated me on all the departmental politics and players. But her favorite subject, by far, was Professor Eric Haynes. Unprompted, she recited his courses, office hours, publications, and current areas of interest. She also delighted in announcing their twice weekly, thirty minute meetings at a time reserved especially for her. She was legal so he was no R. Kelly but, like Robert, he might not see anything wrong with a little bump and grind. I had access to a few Merrill interns on campus that I'd already put on the case. They'll report what they uncover within a few days. I'll probably still be marinating in traffic until then.

My hip buzzed and I answered. "This is Timo."

"Boy, stop trying to sound all official. You know it's me."

"Giovanni?"

"Timo, quit playing. You've had my number programmed into your phone for five years."

She had me there. Even had her own ringtone. I lied to the end. "My bad. I didn't recognize your number. How can I help you?"

"I called to see if you've read any good books lately?"

I cut my eyes to the passenger seat. "Besides that new Walter Mosley joint, not really."

"Okay. I thought you might be able to suggest something for me.

I've been looking for something to read since my mail is running late."

"Tell your boy to grab a Harlequin for you at Barnes and Noble. I hear you two spend a good amount of time there."

"Timo, I considered letting you slide on your macho episode from the other night since you were apparently grieving."

Traffic creeped. I chuckled. "Grieving what?"

"Grieving losing me a second time. I told myself you're not a total cyborg and that everybody makes a fool of themselves when they have regrets."

"All I know is the last thing I said to you was 'call me' and here you are. Don't try to act like you're doing me a favor. Daddy forgives you for trying to make him jealous, sweetheart."

Giovanni continued as if she didn't hear me. "But then when I discovered that you stole my galley copy the night you came by, I changed my mind. You are a total cyborg and I'm not letting you slide."

I stayed cool. "Next time you call me, make sure all the ecstasy is out of your system, okay? What on earth makes you think I took something from your house? If something is missing, the most likely culprit is your kleptomaniac boyfriend. But, when you have a man on leg-lock, the build-up can drive him to do some strange things."

"Slow clap, funnyman. Bravo. Remind me to nominate you for the next NAACP Image Award. Now cut the crap, Timo. I know it was you."

"Proof?"

"My proof is you."

"What?"

"After my editor told me *The Love Manual* had been signed for, I called a neighbor to see if it had been delivered to him by accident. When that didn't check out, I called my editor back and asked him to overnight me another *Love Manual* and to email me a copy of the delivery confirmation receipt."

"So?"

"So I saw that the only word written was 'George', but there was something odd about it."

"Giovanni, the only odd thing is anybody wanting to read that pulp fiction you and Sheila are peddling."

"I'll help you find a woman your speed later. Right now, stay with me."

I could hear D.C. and Luke snickering in my head at that one.

"Timo, I know it was you because of the 'G'."

"Huh?"

"I thought I recognized the handwriting from somewhere but couldn't pull it in. I let it go and went about my day. I happened to stop by the office to grab a client's business card out of my rolodex. While flipping, I came across the business card you gave me when we met and saw that you scribbled a note across the top."

"What'd it say?"

"It said, 'Great meeting you.' The 'G' on your card had the same hook and flare as the 'G' on the UPS receipt."

"That's it?"

"That and the UPS driver that handed you the package swearing you signed for it so he could keep his job if I made a fuss."

There were two ways I could play this, deflated or denial. I chose the river. "I don't know what you're talking about."

"We're past that Timo. Here is your penance. As you may be aware, Sheila has a growing interest in a certain one of your buddies. I need you to get him over to my place at 7pm tonight for dinner."

"Why would I do that?"

"Because you know as well as I do that they are compatible on levels that we never were and it's right to help good people get together."

"Is that all you've got?"

"That and if you and Ricky are even one minute late, my friend at the Atlanta Journal and Constitution will be receiving a call about my ex-boyfriend stealing *The Love Manual* off my porch because the system is that amazing. By the time the story runs, a version of it will be posted on thelovecommitment.com with your name, address, photo, and place of employment."

I waxed indignant. "You wouldn't."

"Let's hope I don't have to. Bye Timo."

The phone clicked. I swerved into the Peach Pass lane and feverishly punched at my keypad.

Chapter Forty One

Timo

"I still can't believe you got tickets. This concert was sold out two hours after tickets went on sale."

The rhythm of my blinker must've hypnotized me. I came clean. "Rick, I didn't exactly get tickets."

Ricky's face looked like he drank three red bulls down too fast. "What?"

He gritted his teeth like Mike Tyson, pre-fight. "Timo, I'm waiting to hear you say '. . . but I got backstage passes' or 'my girl is working the door and is going to let us waltz in'. But you're not saying anything, bruh. And I need to hear you say something soon or we're going to pull over and have one of our dorm room duke sessions."

We hadn't fought in years. But, as I recall, Ricky didn't tire easily. Once we fought for ten minutes after a prank involving him sleeping and mustard. I held him off, but the only way to stop it was to say 'uncle'. When he released his chokehold, he'd barely broken a sweat and wasn't even breathing hard. Judging from his expression, I don't think I would survive another round.

"Dude, it was the only way I could think of to get you dressed and out of the house on such short notice. The truth is Giovanni called and said they want us at her house for dinner by 7. That's the gospel truth."

"Who is *they*?"

"Giovanni and Sheila."

Ricky regarded me while I switched between the creases in his face and the road. Tension slowly transferred from his jaws to his temples.

"Explain to me why Giovanni is calling you after your restraining order routine the other night?"

"I told you. She said they want to have dinner with us."

"Just like that?"

"Just like that."

"What else, Timo."

I felt like Usher. "Okay. Her exact words were that Sheila wants to have dinner with you. But I know Giovanni's also using that as a reason to see me again. She can't resist me, Rick."

Ricky scrutinized me a bit longer, then faced forward and wiped his palms on his pants. I teased. "Bruh, you know you two were practically tongue-kissing at the library."

Ricky didn't break. I went another way. "Hey, it's just dinner. A light evening with two lovely ladies and your wingman at your side. If nothing else, we get good eats and we bounce."

Ricky cross-examined. "Why are you so giddy?"

"Because it's the perfect opportunity to run through their love commitment obstacle course and pass with flying colors. Even though Giovanni knows I swiped it, she'll never think in a million years that I read it. I used to put down all that self-help crap as mental mashed potatoes for losers so she'll never see me coming."

"She knows?"

"That's what she's holding over my head to get you there. But who's the real Mack here?"

"I hear you, dude. I just hope you know what you're doing. Giovanni's no slouch."

"Neither is your boy, Timotheus Barnett. You let me handle Giovanni. You handle Sheila."

"Man, I'm still not with the single mom thing."

"So I've heard. But you've never tasted any of Sheila's cooking. And you know you boys from Tallahassee can eat."

"I'm always down for that. Straight up though, I don't want to lead her on or eat and run. A single mom is a sacred thing."

"Look at you getting all misty about single moms. The way you've been dodging women with kids, I thought you'd be the one trying to stick them all in the gas chamber for crimes against humanity."

"Naw, T. Check it. When I see my parents at school and practice pick those kids up every day, I see dedication and devotion. But when I see single moms do it, they take it to another dimension. They're doing so many things at once that I know it would be easier to do less with the kid, but they don't take the easy way out. I have love for all the single moms holding it down."

"You just don't want to date one because you think you'll lead her on?"

"And because, what if she gets pregnant? Now she's got two kids and two baby daddies to worry about."

"Alright, Dr. Oz. You're over thinking this. It's just dinner."

"No, it's just a game for you. Some of us care how people feel, Timo."

"I care. I care so much that I'm willing to show two beautiful women a fantastic evening who went to all this trouble and cooked dinner for us."

Ricky leaned against the window. His world famous Jack Nicholson smile surfaced. "You say she can cook? Sheila was looking good at the library, Cuz."

I hung a left as the light changed.

Gigi

"G, are you sure they're coming?"

"Positive. Timo said they'd be here at seven on the dot."

Sheila put her hands on her hips. "How did you pull this off?"

"I let Timo know that he owed me big for showing up unannounced the other night. He put up some resistance to save face, but he probably turned his car around in the middle of the street to get another peak at me."

"I hope he has Ricky in his trunk."

I touched her arm. "Don't worry, Sheila. I got this. They'll be here. And if not, after I get a crowfoot and scratch up Timo's car, then we'll enjoy this feast you've prepared."

"Girl, it's just a little cornbread, potato salad, macaroni, greens, Hawaiian chicken, candied yams, and butter bread."

"Don't forget the apple pie."

"It's still in the oven so I didn't count that."

Sheila blew her bangs off her nose and brushed her shoulders. I pretended to throw an oven mitt at her.

"Girl, if the man can stand up after dinner, you'll have to help him to his car. You know you're all that. What's on your mind?"

Sheila leaned against a barstool. "With my company, I can control variables like time and outcomes. If people don't produce or keep their word, I can walk away and choose not to work with them again. If they don't like me, so what? Our relationship is strictly business. Romance is different. First you have to open yourself up to a man so he can see you. Then you hope he likes you enough to stay. Saying he can leave is fine but, if he leaves, he always takes some of you with him. G, I'm not ready for anymore of me to leave right now."

I sat on the adjacent stool. "You know I know. You saw me after Timo. That's what TLC addresses. It keeps things business until both people put their cards on the table. Business can be efficient as well as sweet. You're both. Now give me a hug and let me get ready to enjoy my food while I torture Timo."

We laughed and embraced.

"You don't think this makes me look desperate, Gigi? For real?"

"I think you're stunning and so will Ricky when he walks through that door. Keep in mind, you're in charge. You summoned him to the palace…and he's coming."

Sheila stood. "Let me check that pie."

I spun on the cushion. "And you cook? Girl, he'll be lucky if he remembers his name after waking up from that food coma."

Sheila placed her hand on the oven door handle and pulled. "Diamond loves apple pie."

"From what I heard, she loves Mr. Ricky, too."

"Don't start that. You know I don't want her getting used to anybody that won't be around."

"Who would that be Sheila? You haven't dated anybody since Steve."

Sheila let the oven door slam shut. "That's precisely why. If her own father isn't reliable, who can I trust with her heart?"

"Don't you hide behind that child, Sheila. We're talking about your heart here. No risk, no reward. You know that."

"I know. But I'd take a safe bet right about now."

"Honey, safe bets don't look like Ricky."

It was Sheila who waved the oven mitt this time. "Girl, strong, well read, and buns of steel? What am I thinking?"

"Ricky can wear a pair of jeans, Sheila."

Sheila stood up straight and took a whiff. "Make me drop this pie and fill up both my hands."

I dipped my chin. "Glad to see you back in business."

Sheila winked. "By the way, did you ever figure out what happened to that delivery?"

"Yeah, I tracked it down. Some kid in the neighborhood pranked the UPS carrier, pretended to be my child, and chicken-scratched my last name. He couldn't even write in cursive so I doubt if he can read. Unless the person is serious and mature, the book is of no value and is under no threat. Maybe when he grows up he'll read it but, by then, we'll be senior citizens."

"Speak for yourself, Madea."

Sheila snickered and motioned toward the coffee table. "Think we should hide that?"

I grinned and shook my head. "It's safe. Besides, it'll be a conversation starter."

Chapter Forty Two

Timo

I hit the doorbell at 6:59 with twenty-two seconds to spare. Ricky questioned me about jumping five steps at once, but I told him it was an inside joke.

Giovanni answered the door smelling edible. She wore a multicolored sundress with braided, leather sandals and freshly painted toenails. I took a bite into her with my eyes.

"Gentlemen, welcome. So good of you to arrive on time. And with flowers."

I inhaled their fragrance. "Not for you, for the house. May we come in?"

She alleged thinking it over. "I suppose."

Giovanni stepped aside and spoke to Ricky. "Roses? For the house, too?"

"Hello, Giovanni. One is for you. The rest are for Sheila."

Ricky handed Giovanni the rose. She leaned in as if to inhale. "I heard what you said about me having a 'setup' look in my eyes."

Ricky cut a hard glance at me in speechless disbelief. I shrugged and retreated into the floral arrangement. Giovanni continued. "You were right. I'm trying to set you up with the woman of your dreams. So don't screw this up or I'll have two things I'm holding against you."

With that, she smelled her rose and raised her voice. "Gentleman, follow me please."

We sat down and sunk into the plush ensemble. The vapor from the pot liquor already had me inebriated and Ricky had licked his lips more than once. Giovanni excused herself to alert Sheila of our arrival. It was a supremely girly thing to make men wait, but I loved to play the game and relished the thrill of the chase.

The cover on the *Essence* magazine hadn't changed since my last visit but there had been an addition to the coffee table reading material.

Ricky saw it first and whispered a head gesture. "Timo."

I nodded. "Trying to mess with me."

"That's not our copy, is it?"

I heard footsteps coming toward us. "Uh-uh. Another one. I'll tell you about it."

We stood to receive Giovanni and an approaching silhouette. Sheila emerged from the hallway wearing a purple cloth dress that flowed and hugged in all the right places. The folds at her neck supplied a hint of cleavage, but that was more than enough to make Ricky trip on the coffee table trying to move toward her.

"These are for you."

"Thank you, Ricky. How sweet. Let me find some water."

It was a sheer test of will to keep from following her into the kitchen with my eyes. Ricky failed. But there was no need. Like Mos Def said, Sheila had so much booty you could see it from the front.

Giovanni shot Ricky the 'ok' sign and sneered at me. I extended my hand. "You know these are for you."

She accepted the flowers. "I know. I was just waiting for you to grow up and give them to me. Make yourselves comfortable. We'll be with you shortly."

Giovanni joined Sheila in the kitchen and, at that moment, I realized how Helen of Troy launched a thousand ships. Any man around her for any length of time would do anything to make her happy. Her kicking me out saved me from premature surrender.

The girls filled vases and traded giggles at the sink while we contorted our faces and shook our heads. Maybe men were little boys in grown up bodies, because we both wanted to eat and fall asleep on mama tonight.

"We're ready guys."

Sheila's tone was soft and commanding. Ricky and I fought to our feet like kindergarteners competing for the prize of first one standing. We watched as the ladies set the table and populated the top with uncovered dishes. I envisioned myself in a Batman movie waddling out afterwards with an umbrella like the Penguin. If they let us hit that couch after dinner, good money said we wouldn't get up until morning.

Ricky and I unbuttoned our blazers and took our chances.

Chapter Forty Three

Gigi

"Sheila, did you see how he handed you those roses? I thought he picked them himself the way he stood at attention."

Sheila filled the vase. "You'd be wise to check your bushes before they leave."

"I will. Meanwhile, you'd better feed that man or he's going to put you on a plate with some syrup and start sopping."

The boys stood by our chairs until we were ready to be seated. Ricky pulled Sheila's chair out and Timo followed suit. Where was all this chivalry coming from? Before I knew it, we were bowing our head for grace.

"Thank you Lord for this bounty and for the hands that prepared it. We pray that our conversation will be as delightful as the food and the company. In your name, Amen."

I spread my napkin across my lap. "That was a lovely prayer, Ricky. Where do you fellowship?"

"Creekside, in South Fulton. It's a bit far, but they do a lot of outreach. One of my students was always talking about his church and what they did for the youth. I decided to visit and have been a member of the outreach team ever since."

"You hear that Sheila? Sheila does outreach with her church, too. Isn't that right Sheila?"

Sheila put some bread into her mouth and nodded. Timo spoke while dishing helpings onto his plate. "Ricky's a regular Brother Teresa. If he didn't have to work, he'd probably be running a soup kitchen right now. He says all the blessings at our Thursday guy nights. Isn't that right, Rick?"

Ricky found the bread basket and imitated Sheila. Timo changed course. "Sheila, nice job on the website. I hear you're up to a million hits now?"

Sheila swallowed. "Thanks. All in a day's work. We're targeting African American women primarily, but women from all ethnicities all over the country are responding to the concept."

Timo poured lemonade into his glass. "You should be getting calls from some major sponsors pretty soon; especially with the TV exposure."

Sheila wiped her mouth. "We already have. Gigi asked the publishing house to recommend some attorneys to handle that feature. We've received two packets in the mail from advertising firms as of yesterday."

I interjected. "Speaking of mail, did you boys get a chance to look at the galley copy of *The Love Manual*?"

Both Timo and Ricky stopped mid-chew. I rescued them. "It's on the coffee table. I thought you might have skimmed it while you were waiting."

Timo responded and Ricky finger-wiped his hairline. "We noticed it right before you two came out, but we didn't get a chance to read it. However, we did catch the interview. That's why I came by the other night; before the good doctor interrupted the conversation."

Ricky held up his fork. "These yams are delicious. I don't know if the cinnamon is in the syrup or on these dinner rolls, but what I'm eating will make you talk back to your mama."

Sheila cooed. "Thank you."

I elaborated. "Ricky, everything you eat here tonight was made from scratch by that lady right there."

Ricky lifted his glass. "My sincere compliments to the chef."

Sheila touched his glass and they drank together.

Timo seized the silence. "Before the Nutty Professor barged in, all I wanted to clarify is that I didn't leave you, you left me."

"No, I threw you out. There's a difference."

"On the show it sounded like I was this trifling brother who didn't have his stuff together."

"You said it. Look Timo, the truth is that you told me you weren't ready for marriage and I didn't accept it."

"That we agree on."

I finished. "So now I accept it and I've moved on. Not to mention I haven't seen or heard from you in three years."

Ricky grabbed a dish. "And these greens are seasoned to perfection. You sure these aren't Glory Greens?"

Sheila laughed. I didn't. Neither did Timo. But we both saw that it was time to take a break.

"Timo I will walk with you down memory lane after dinner. Right now, let's agree to table that for later."

Timo nodded. "These greens really are the bomb. And that Hawaiian chicken? Falling off the bone, girl."

Sheila soaked in the praise of both men. As much as I hate to admit it, women do need that. And when Timo was on, he could make a woman feel like she'd had a backrub, foot massage, and mental orgasm without ever being touched. And if Ricky was anything like him, he had those super powers, too. So I decided to bring some balance to the Force.

Chapter Forty Four

Timo

Giovanni oozed apathy about her on-camera antics. I bided my time until the setting was more conducive for my plan to work. Still Giovanni's stubbornness and her scent were making that difficult. Both enticed me to bite her. I settled for the butter bread and chicken breast.

Giovanni put the wheels in motion. "So Ricky, I know about Timo and Sheila but not very much about you. What's your story?"

Sheila dabbed her mouth and shot a Vulcan death stare across the table. Giovanni raised her chin and focused more intently on Ricky.

"Well, you know I'm from Tallahassee and went to FAMU. I have a brother and a sister still there along with my parents. They don't live with my parents, just in town. My sister's married with a child, Karen. My brother is divorced with two boys, Devin and Delon. Me? Never married, no kids."

I lent a hand. "But you love kids."

"Kind of hard not to."

Giovanni's cheekbones showed her appreciation. "Sheila says Diamond was all over you at the library last week."

Ricky lit up. "Where is Diamond?"

Sheila responded. "She's with Ms. C., a friend of ours with kids her age."

Ricky held her gaze. "Diamond's a beautiful girl, and quick. Very articulate. She's going places. No secret where she gets that from."

Sheila blushed. "For some reason she's recently developed an interest in soccer."

"We may have discussed her coming to a game this season, with your permission of course."

Giovanni ran interference. "So, Ricky, did you play soccer?"

Ricky took the hint. Back on the auction block. "I did. My dad was a high school P.E. teacher and soccer coach for thirty years. I grew up playing before soccer became a popular sport in the States. You can imagine that I was the only black kid on most of my teams. But my dad always said that soccer taught discipline, patience, and perseverance. You could run up and down that field for twenty minutes just to set up one shot. A good game might have a score of 1-0 for an hour's worth of play."

I shook my head. "That's not enough scoring for me. I need fast-paced action for my sporting entertainment."

Ricky gestured toward me with his hands. "Like yours truly, most Americans are spoiled by high-flying dunks and towering homeruns wrapped in media magic. Outside the U.S., everybody plays soccer and fans appreciate the degree of skill possessed by the best players."

I rejoined. "If we were in Lithuania, that'd be swell. But we're in the ATL, and black people don't like all that running for nothing. I need some return on my time investment."

Giovanni touched my forearm. "Can you let Ricky tell his own story?"

I took a sip of lemonade in tacit compliance.

Ricky resumed. "Since I attended an all-black high school, rustling up a team was tough. On top of that, soccer is a winter sport in Florida, so getting people to run back and forth or sit in the stands in the cold for a low scoring game was another chore."

Sheila responded. "But you must've loved playing?"

"Somewhere between summer youth leagues and cold high school seasons was the time my dad and I spent speaking the same language. I understand how important that time was for me, so it's meaningful when I can share some of that with my team."

Giovanni pried. "Any old girlfriends?"

I saw Sheila jerk and Giovanni's leg jump under the table. Giovanni titled her head in Sheila's direction. "Don't act like you don't want to know."

Ricky held up his hands. "It's alright. A couple."

I beat my chest when I heard his humble reply. "A couple? That's like saying Kim Kardashian has a couple of old pairs of shoes."

"Okay then, a few."

Ricky's look indicated that I had inched across the player-hater line. "My bad, Fabio."

The facetious apology went unanswered. I tried to redeem myself. "How many old girlfriends does the professor have?"

Giovanni sighed. "You just couldn't wait."

"We agreed to table the talk show discussion, not Dr. Doolittle. Oh, I get it. You get to drill Ricky with question after question but I can't ask any?"

Giovanni's silence was a signal that I finally had Sonny Liston tired. Time for the rope-a-dope. "I have a better idea. Why don't we step outside and give these two a little privacy so they can get better acquainted?"

Her lips were pinned shut. To protest would have been awkward, since that was the stated intent of the dinner. Giovanni glared at me, then looked to Sheila. "Fine. We can talk on the porch."

I pulled out her chair. "Ricky don't eat up all that apple pie, bruh. I'll be back for my piece."

As she rose, Giovanni and Sheila communicated through visual telepathy. When it ended, I followed Giovanni to the door. This time the small of her back fell prey to my hand guiding her onto the porch.

Chapter Forty Five

Gigi

You're on your *own, girl. Just relax and be yourself.* Sheila's expression told me she got the message. Strangely, I felt she sent me the same one as I stood. I could feel Timo's smirk radiating through the palm of his hand. I waited until the door closed.

"Hands off Captain Touchy."

"What's wrong? Irony too much for you?"

"It's not ironic. I just know how your mind works."

"I see. You can dish it..."

"Oh, I can take it."

Timo's voice grew husky. "Don't I know? But since you mentioned it, how're you holding up with that?"

"With what?"

"Your vow."

"Did Sheila tell you that, too?"

"No, you did...on national TV."

"No, I didn't."

"You said that before a love commitment is established, sex interferes with rational judgment. Since I don't see a ring on your finger and I didn't read about it in the paper, I presume you and Dr. Jekyll aren't doing the do."

"Mind your own business, Timo."

"My bad. I just had a question about how you said sex releases some kind of chemical."

"Oxytocin."

"Yeah. And that creates an emotional bond."

I lifted my feet to buy processing time. Timo did the same and the porch swing swung into action.

He cheesed. "Didn't think I was listening, huh? I told you I had to talk to you about the broadcast."

"What about it?"

"Well, according to your system, you and I have released so much oxytocin that we're bonded for life."

I stopped the swing. "I thought there might be hope for you. Wrong again."

"So what do you really know about this Poindexter? Do you love him?"

He caught me off guard. It was fight or flight. I fought. "If you know so much about The Love Commitment, you should know that we're in the Verification Phase, checking out what we think and want."

"But do you love him?"

He kept hammering. I couldn't think of a way to spin this one. "Almost."

"Almost isn't an answer. It's either 'yes' or 'no'."

I stood over Timo to regain my footing. "It's still forming. But that brings up a good point. Men have used love against women for centuries and mostly because we think we're in control of it."

"What are you talking about?"

"Usually women are the ones refusing 'practical' marriages by demanding that the flames of romantic love consume every encounter. But when things go wrong or lovers are incompatible, it's generally the practical things that break down. Why not make sure the practical things are there first, then allow love to form? That's what I'm doing. It's like my girl Dana Gilmore says, 'I should've never put my heart in my mind's position'. So don't try to bring that weak game you ran on me for three years in my face again. I appreciate you getting Ricky here, but that's all you get from me."

Timo stood and my eyes spread across his chest for what felt like an eternity. "Alright. Verification Phase. Well, do you know who Eric dated while we dated? Do you know how he spends his days? Where is he now and why isn't he here instead of me?"

I stepped back. "I know what he's told me so far and, if I need more, I'll ask. But for your information, he's working on a book and he stays in his office weeknights so he can finish by the summer's end."

"So you only see him on the weekend?"

"Mostly. But that's fine with me. And why am I telling you all this anyway?"

"Because, like it or not, I'm the closest man to you in your life."

I couldn't quickly dismiss Timo's comeback and it boiled my blood; so I dismissed the need to. "I'm going in the backdoor to gather some information. You can do whatever you want."

"You mean eavesdrop?"

I pulled out my key ring and jingled it.

"When in Rome don't look a gift horse in the mouth, or something like that. Lead the way, Cleopatra Jones. I'm right behind you."

Chapter Forty Six

Timo

The way Giovanni turned the lock without making a sound should have instantly qualified her for cat burglar of the year. I felt my pocket for the house key, just to make sure I wouldn't be her next victim.

She put her index finger over her lips and tiptoed through the laundry room. I left the door slightly ajar to avoid blowing our cover. In the next room, giggling and light banter filled the air. We cracked the adjoining door and got a rear view of them still at the table. I crouched down on all fours and stuck my head across the threshold for better acoustics.

"Ricky I didn't know you were so well traveled."

"I still have tons of places I want to see. But I really want to tour the Underground Railroad stations from here to Canada one summer."

"That would be amazing. I'd love to do that with Diamond but I could never get away for that long."

Why not? You're the boss, right?"

"True, but I also work on billable hours so if I don't work, I don't get paid."

"I'm just saying that a trip like that would be priceless, even worth missing a few paychecks to me."

Ricky pushed his plate aside and continued. "You might as well think about it. It would kill two birds with one stone."

"What two birds?"

"It would let you see the stations and it would keep the matchmakers happy."

"Who? Gigi and Timo?"

"Who else?"

"Sorry. I mentioned you a few times to Gigi and the rest is history."

Ricky blushed. "Don't be sorry about that. I told Timo a few things about you, too. So we're even."

Sheila chuckled.

Ricky returned the gesture and inquired. "What's so funny?"

She covered her brows with her hand. "I don't believe I'm telling you this, but I usually don't go for Humanities majors."

"Not Alpha-Male enough for you, huh?"

"No, it's just that Diamond's dad was a History major and he hasn't been very reliable."

"Oh, is that all? Well you'll be pleased to know that I was a Social Studies Major, which is like history, geography, and current events rolled up into one. I'd say that makes me at least three times as reliable as a plain old History major."

Ricky surprised me with his answer. I was proud of my boy. Giovanni pressed her lips together and put her index finger up again.

"So Sheila, if you could go anywhere in the world, where would it be?"

Sheila grazed Ricky's bicep. "Nobody's ever asked me that question."

"Take your time. No rush."

Sheila suppressed a smile by looking up and to the left. "Hmmm. I think it would have to be the Maldives."

"Excellent choice. How come?"

"Pictures of the islands are so beautiful and the water looks so blue and clear."

"We need to get you there before the hurricanes and tsunamis wash them away."

Giovanni whispered to me. "He said 'we'."

I put my fist over my mouth. "I know, I know."

In the exhilaration, I lost my balance and fell in slow motion against the washing machine.

Sheila jumped. "Gigi?"

Giovanni came out with her hands up. "We're here Sheila. Come on, Timo."

I got up brushing my hands like Deputy Barney Fife.

Ricky held his response until I'd made it to the table. "Timo? Boy you're wild."

I squinted with the sour face. "Huh? Man, I came in here to get you. We gotta roll. Sheila baby, everything was beautiful. Can I get a big piece of that pie to go?"

Sheila swiveled her neck from Timo to Giovanni and loud-laughed. "You two are a trip."

Giovanni was drafted to my side. "Just making sure you're alright, girl."

Sheila put both hands on her hips. "And what were you two doing, all sweaty, in the laundry room?"

Giovanni and I wiped our faces at the same time. "Nothing."

Sheila held her pose. "Uh-huh. I'll deal with you later, Ms. Thang. Right now let me cut these men some pie so they can make their appointment. Ricky, your piece will be much bigger than his."

I pouted. Ricky stood up. "Right is right, bruh. Pay karma now or pay it later."

We said our goodbyes at the door. After giving Ricky an energetic hug, Sheila handed him an aluminum pie plate and me a napkin. Ricky promised to call while Giovanni threw me an old lady, pat-back hug. She knew I hated that. I didn't even say goodbye when we walked out.

Chapter Forty Seven

Timo

We drove in silence for five stop signs. Ricky waved the aluminum tray near my nose with exaggerated sounds. "I might get a stomach ache eating this whole pie by myself."

The empire struck back. "I see you got over eating and running."

"Meaning?"

"Meaning that on the way here, you had a stake in your pocket to stab any single mom that came near you. Now you're out there yapping like Dick Gregory doing standup. What changed?"

"Timo man, I really had a good time with her. That doesn't mean I'm cool with the single mom thing, because I'm not. But I'm cool with Sheila and I'm cool with Diamond so, who knows?"

"'Who knows?' is not the question to ask about...what were your words? 'A single mom is a sacred thing.' If I didn't know any better, I'd think Slick Rick the Ruler was back trying to get some butter bean."

"You're just mad because I had a good time and Giovanni treated you like a wet food stamp."

"Shut up, Ricky."

"Don't run off the road, Timo. Your lips are hanging."

I brooded for a moment longer. Ricky patronized me. "Did Giovanni hurt your feelings again? My fault, bruh. I forgot how delicate you are about matters of the heart."

I grinned from ear to ear. It's mindboggling to women why guys interpret male insensitivity as humor, but we do. Perhaps it's as much a learned response as crying is for them.

I came around. "Not that I was listening…"

"Timo, you need to stop lying. You almost fell through the wall trying to take notes."

"It was her idea. Her house, her key, her rules."

"I hope you heard a few things to strengthen your rap game."

"Off the record, I'll give you your props. You had Sheila in there ready to break out the Luther Vandross. She floated across the room like Wendy after Peter Pan sprinkled that pixie dust in her face. I can't leave you alone five minutes without you getting mannish."

"Me? What about you on the front porch? I thought I might need to break up the action on that swing."

"Naw, Rick. Just getting in her head. That's all."

"About what?"

"How she's entertaining me and her man is unaccounted for."

"What'd she say?"

"That he works late every weeknight."

Ricky pointed at me. "Remember that dude on TV the other night? That got gaffled by his old lady?"

"Oh, yeah. That bank teller who told his wife he works late closing up? That fool ran a red light one night with his other chick in the car…"

I started laughing so Ricky picked up. "… and the cops mailed the picture to his house. By the time he got home that day, his wife and furniture were in a U-haul headed to her parents. But she did leave him a parting gift."

I took a breath. "What?"

"She blew up pictures of him with the girl and super-glued them to all the walls."

I nursed a cramp in my side and slowed for pedestrians in the crosswalk. "I'm telling you Rick, that dude is playing Giovanni the same way."

"How do you know?"

"I sense it, hard. Remember when I told you that cat, Ray, was beating on Lashell?"

"Yeah, and you were jealous that he married your high school sweetheart."

"But was I right?"

"Unfortunately."

"Rick, I've got that same feeling here."

"Man, I can see your hunch with Ray. That dude was big and didn't smile at all. But the way you describe your scholarly nemesis, he's the exact opposite."

"So he's a pretty boy. Pretty boys lie and they definitely cheat."

"Are you hating on that man? What's it to you anyway? You said you're only out for revenge."

I took the fifth. Ricky nodded. "Oh, I forgot. Green-eyed monster never dies. Just don't let that black mascara run all over the pillowcases tonight."

My phone buzzed. I looked down and considered the poetry of the glowing, green screen. I raised an index finger to Ricky. "Just the call I've been waiting for."

Gigi

"Sheila you didn't have to give them the whole pie."

"Why not? You didn't deserve any. Back there snooping like Easy Rawlings. And what were you and Timo doing that he had to come in wiping his hands?"

"Don't even try it. I heard you two out here like Regina Belle and Peabo Bryson."

"So you *were* snooping?"

"Like I said, I was watching your back."

"Seems to me like Timo was watching yours."

"Girl, you know that's a B.C. date. Besides, I got a man."

"Okay, I'm just telling you what I smell."

"What?"

"That natural mystic in the air when you two are together."

"Not hardly. Girl, let's bust these suds so you can get Diamond into bed."

She tied the apron around her waist. "I cook, you wash. I rinse, you dry. Deal?"

"You know I have no problem with that."

Sheila rinsed the glasses and hung them on the dish rack. "You still haven't told me what all that porch snuggling was about."

"That was nothing. Timo being Timo. All in my business about Eric, trying to raise doubts."

"About?"

"Eric. Like what do I really know about him and why we don't spend that much time together?"

"To tell you the truth G, I wonder that, too. I know he's working on something, but new love is supposed to be spontaneous and constant."

"It's supposed to be, but it's still early on. And since we agreed to wait for sex, that chills a lot of the frenzy for me."

Sheila rinsed the forks. "Not for me. Girl, I don't care if we're talking about world peace. I'm thinking about getting some."

"Sheila, it's like that?"

"Is it like that? Remember, while you were leg in leg with Timo, I was raising Diamond. That was enough for then, but now I'm ready to make up for lost time. When Ricky asked me where I wanted to go, the Maldives was my second choice."

"What was the first?"

"His place."

I kept scrubbing plates. "Ooh, mamasita. Ants in your pants is not good. Better pump your brakes."

"You're gonna have to pray me through on this one because I already saw myself letting the seat down in a daydream."

I dried my hands and leaned against the sink. "Do you want this man?"

"I just told you that."

"No, I'm serious. Do you really want this man? Can you see yourself married to him—to have and to hold, in sickness and in health, for richer or poorer?"

Sheila turned off the water. "Yes."

"Then you're going to have to get control of your hormones. Sheila, you and I both know that sex too soon will ruin a love commitment. There are too many variables."

"Gigi, it sounded good when we were coming up with the concept, but that tingling changes things."

I put my hand on her shoulder. "That's why we have to stick to the script. It's the only way women will be able to come together. But if *we* don't do it, why in the world would they do it? It's just like religion. When people see hypocrites, they blame the system, not the hypocrite. This is bigger than us. I know that's a heavy load to carry, but if we have to, we'll become roommates again so we can help each other maintain."

"Child, that man moves something up on the inside of me. Made me have a Jill Scott moment while I was cutting that pie."

"Alright. But I hope you didn't drip any of that love juice in my yams."

"Honey, it was airborne. Hormones were flying all over the place."

I mumbled. "That doesn't sound like the Holy Ghost to me."

"No, but it did feel like fire shut up in my bones."

We both needed the laugh. Sheila took off her apron. "Gigi, I think I might have to do Plan B and have a car waiting on engagement party night."

"I hear you, girl. I'm sure a lot of women will choose that route. But y'all better make sure that the love commitment is really there. If sex is the main event, trouble will be waiting in the next round."

"Look who's talking. You stored up enough to last you a good while."

"See, you're wrong. I have needs, too. But one of my needs is to not be divorced after two years because I married the sex instead of the man."

Sheila interlocked her fingers. "You don't have to worry about that. Even though I'm combustible right now, any man I bring into my bed has to love and accept me and my child."

"Well you might want to find that out before you buy satin sheets."

"Ricky adores Diamond."

"I agree. Ricky also likes kids, in general. That doesn't mean he's asking to be Diamond's new daddy. Next time you two get together, you probably need to get his take on blended families."

Sheila wiped the tabletop. "Girl, be glad it's only you Eric has to think about."

She sensed my unspoken hesitation. "What, G?"

"I can't explain it. I didn't let on with Timo, but he was right. I do wonder why Eric doesn't call me as much as I think he should. We text, but it's pretty predictable."

Sheila straightened up. "Predictable is good, right? Especially in a love commitment?"

"Most of the time. But a love commitment still needs that spice. Those spontaneous, wild, sweet gestures that make courting what it's supposed to be."

"And you don't feel that from him?"

"I did when we met and again when he found me at the house, but not as much these last few weeks."

"You think something's changed?"

"All I know about is his research."

"Any new women on the scene?"

"Timo hinted at that, too. To be honest Sheila, I really wouldn't know."

"Well girl, you remember when we were kids and Jenny Peters tried to move in on Derrick?"

"Sheila that was 8th grade."

"Uh-huh. Well she tried to share her sandwiches with him during lunch period. Child, I went home and made that boy a sandwich he would never forget and brought it to his house after school? Let's just say I never had to worry about Jenny Peters and Derrick again, and neither did he."

"But Sheila, I can't cook like you."

"I'm not talking about cooking, I'm talking about courting... on both ends. If TLC works for both men and women, then the man should get his share of being wooed, too."

At that moment my phone rang. All this talk of Eric must have conjured him up from his books and computer screen. The universe is always conspiring to give us what we need precisely when we need it.

Sheila craned her neck to see. "Who's that?"

I checked the Caller ID and allowed the phone to ring once more. "I don't recognize the number. It's the Emory area code though. And I only know one person who'd be calling me from that location."

I'd hoped, but couldn't truly say I expected Eric to call. You might have thought I was leading the praise dance at Sheila's church the way I jumped up and down. The phone rang a third time. Despite sporting a classic Halle Berry haircut since college, I took a deep breath and flung imaginary locks over my shoulder when I answered."

"Hello?"

A musical tone responded. "Hello, Giovanni. How are you?"

"Storie?"

"I apologize for the lateness of the hour. Did I wake you?"

"No, it's just that..." I shook my head at Sheila. "Sorry. I thought you were someone else."

"That's quite all right. Walters and I are passing through town and decided to lodge at the house this evening."

"That's great. The cleaning crew you hired keeps the place in immaculate condition."

"Walters remarked not five minutes ago about that very thing."

I wondered about the call but didn't ask outright. "How long are you in town?"

"That partially explains my bothering you. We are headed to Savannah tomorrow morning but I would very much like to speak with you tonight if you are available."

"Sheila and I just finished dinner and the dishes."

"Wonderful. Bring her as well. We can have after dinner tea and pastries."

I repeated Storie's words. "Tea and pastries?"

Sheila vigorously nodded her head. I flashbacked to Sheila hovering over the hors d'oeuvres at Storie's Christmas party. "Okay, we'll be there in about thirty minutes."

"Perfect. We will see you then. Goodbye, Dear."

Chapter Forty Eight

Timo

"Whatchu got for me Monty?"

"Mr. B., I asked around about that business and found out that he does meet with her three times a week and sometimes she's up in his office late, like ten or eleven."

"What's your source?"

"My boy from Decatur is part of the second shift cleaning crew and he sees her up there making copies and chit-chatting with your guy all the time."

I felt Ricky's silent interrogation on the side of my face. The light turned green and my foot obeyed. "Is that it?"

"The other night, he said he had to repaint the bathroom walls due to some scribbling about the Dean and where he could stick next year's tuition hike, when he overheard your guy and Candace arguing outside the door."

"About what?"

"My boy Craig said they were fussing about not spending enough time together and how his mind has been occupied lately instead of on her."

"What happened next?"

"Craig said she went into the girl's bathroom and your guy went back to his office. Craig peeked out to see if the coast was clear and hit the stairwell."

"One last thing, Monty. How did you come by all this information so fast?"

"Easy. When you called me and mentioned Candace, I knew exactly who you were talking about because half the bruhs in my frat have been chasing her since freshman year. But of all the guys I know, Craig has the biggest crush on her. So he'd ask me if I knew her when I came home on weekends. I told him what I knew and he told me how he flirted with her from time to time while emptying the trash on that floor. So all I had to do was get Craig an invitation to our next frat party and promise to introduce him to Candace. Craig sung like a canary. I personally think he would've signed an affidavit to get that close to her. But a deal's a deal, right Mr. B.?"

I had to admire the future stockbroker. "Right. You'll have your offer letter by the end of the week."

"Thanks Mr. B. Oh, could you send it to my house on Merrill stationery? I want my moms to open it when I go home this weekend."

"Sure thing. I'll holler at you, Monty. Peace."

I closed the phone and rehearsed what Craig told Monty. Ricky tapped his upper lip. "What're you going to do?"

I hunched my shoulders. "I haven't decided, but I know that Giovanni deserves better."

Satisfaction seeped down Ricky's face. Maybe Sheila's smorgasbord had begun working its magic. "Took you three years, but Sir Lancelot is finally ready for battle."

"Whatever. I'm just saying if Professor X wants to be a player, he can find somebody else for that."

Ricky adjusted his pitch to mimic Scarlet O'Hara. "Why Timo, I do believe the touch of love has transformed you into a gentleman."

I snorted and turned away, trying my best to hide the resonance of Ricky's words. I turned back. He was still there. The silence was both loud and merciful until I smothered it.

"Gentleman or not, why do I feel like I got hustled by Monty?"

"Because you thought you had the upper hand when you didn't. You probably promised him that job when you knew he was going to get it anyway. Am I right?"

Protruding my lips was as good as a full confession. "Your point?"

"So he gave you something he already had. It was an even trade. If you ask me, you got much more out of the deal."

I pulled into the apartment lot and shifted into park. "Yeah, an apprentice who'll take my job in a few years and a woman who'll hate me even more when I tell her something for her own good."

Gigi

We talked about Ricky and Eric the whole way there. Sheila did most of the talking, but the fact that Eric hadn't called was all I could think about. Sheila practically carried on the conversation by herself. Good thing. If she had asked me a question that required more than 'uh-huh' or a giggle, my acknowledgement of drifting would have preceded a request for Sheila to repeat herself. And Sheila hated to repeat herself.

When we reached Storie's place it was about 10pm. She left the outside light on and I pulled past Captain Burns' grave to appease my passenger.

Sheila changed subjects when the car stopped. "Did Storie say what she wanted?"

"No. But I figure she wants an update on any interested buyers."

"Are there any?"

"Not really. Aside from Eric, a retired couple scheduled an appointment but the stairs were too steep for them. The prequalification letter screens out people who can't buy but like to play peek-a-boo while realtors burn up their gas. And since I'm showing this one myself, you know I'm conserving that super unleaded."

No sooner than we hit the sidewalk, the front door opened and a Zulu hunter walked to the edge of the steps with his hand extended. "Welcome ladies. Thank you for coming on such short notice."

I think I may have curtsied in return and Sheila grabbed his fingers with both hands as he guided us in from the night.

Walters' mellifluous voice soothed all thoughts of any other man. "Storie is in the parlor. Please, this way."

Storie greeted us both with big hugs and let her eyes linger on Walters as if she hadn't seen him for days. He brought us tea and pastries on an actual silver platter and made sure we had everything we needed. If Chippendales had a middle-aged companion service, dressed them in business casual, and taught them to love on women until their hearts ached, he would be their most requested escort.

Walters bowed. "Ladies, if you will excuse me. I am the designated driver tomorrow so I will bid you adieu." He blew Storie a soft kiss and strolled out leaving a manly redolence behind.

We both beheld Storie. She paused to honor our admiration. After our smiles faded, I spoke. "Storie, we haven't had much movement on the house. I was so sure it would be gone by now."

"Giovanni, considering the market, a property in this range will take at least a year to choose its new owner."

Sheila and I nibbled on the warm strawberry filling, thinking about what Storie meant.

I braved. "How so?"

Storie brought her tea down. "Homes like this can only be purchased by the right people. There are many who have driven by or looked at the listing, but they simply may not be the choice of the house. Beyond price, the history and features of the home demand someone with suitable character and intentions to inhabit and use it properly."

Sheila entered the exchange. "What's the proper use?"

"I couldn't say exactly, my Dear. For us, it was to restore and carve out its intended beauty from the original substance. For other owners, it may have been to raise a family or to shelter wayward travelers. Like people, the destiny of a property is fluid and evolves in the same way its owners evolve."

Sheila followed her question. "Do you believe houses help shape people's destinies?"

"Certainly. Social scientists have been writing for ages about the effect of environment on mental and social development. The stimuli in one's environment lead the maturation process in appreciable ways."

I interjected. "So you think growing up in this house and then returning to it affected who you are as a person?"

"Yes, Giovanni. This house has done that for all of us. It has given me many gifts…as it has you."

Sheila and I gawked at each other and then at Storie.

Storie sipped her tea and continued. "I viewed the broadcast last week and surmised that the house had chosen you to deliver the Black Victorian principles to the modern world through your *Love Manual*."

Sheila blurted. "You knew about it?"

"Yes. I knew where it was but had never seen it. What I understand of it is from my mother. She told me all about it and the principles it contains. And she never ceased to talk about my great, great grandmother."

"Dido Lindsay was your great, great grandmother?" Sheila started to pick up her tea and decided against it. "I'm somewhere between embarrassed and confused."

Storie soothed us both. "Not to worry. I was not selected to bestow this gift. You were. All of the matriarchs in my family fulfilled their roles. But it was not ours to walk this next mile of the journey. It was yours. This is why I asked you to come."

I reached out for Storie's hand. "Thank you for being so splendid.

We were scared you would be upset if you knew we found the principles in the tunnels."

Storie twinkled. "I sensed you had a part to play when we met in this room on your birthday. It was clear to me after we shared over the next year and when my work here came to an end. Giovanni, the house even chose you as its realtor."

It was a lot to digest. I half understood what Storie said with reservations. "Do you feel like we violated your trust by taking your family's principles to the world instead of you being the one to do it?"

Her mannerisms were kind. "No. My life has been magnificent. I have no need for envy. But I do believe I am to share a key insight with you."

Sheila and I both bobbed our heads.

"When I heard you speak on television about the celibate period, I did not hear the vital ingredient that allows this approach to succeed."

Sheila asked without realizing. "What?"

"An enormous amount of attentiveness and affection. Without this, 'the love commitment' as you call it, will seldom materialize due to most men's sexual frustration."

Storie's observations were unexpected and welcome. I recalled the interview. "So that's what Sister Vanessa was getting at with her statement about driving the man to infidelity?"

"So it was. The man of yesterday had more restraint because the times reflected that level of discipline. He could wait because waiting was woven into the fabric of society. However, the modern man has freedom to your, and his own, detriment. He sees waiting as an injury because of the visual and physical stimulation his environment supplies. Similar to an addiction, he must be stabilized through consistent and quality affection."

Sheila put her tea and pastry onto the table. "Break it down so it will forever be broken."

Storie flitted a chuckle. "When you decide that he is the man for you, hug him, kiss him, hold his hand, listen to him, rub his arm, write him notes, cook for him. But, most of all, support him and build him up. Never say things to tear him down, in public or in private. Confide in him and allow him to confide in you without fear. If you give these gifts to your man, you will never lose them; for the more you give, the more you have. This kind of love between black men and women will literally change the world and rebuild our families."

Storie stood and brushed the crumbs from her nightgown. "I have said enough. You all know what to do. And if not immediately, you will soon. Now if you'll excuse me, I need to go put that man to bed."

Neither of us had a response. Storie graced us with a knowing look. "Until you can feed your man a full meal, you must give him snacks as often as possible...or you will find him binging at another woman's table. Do keep me posted, Giovanni. Goodnight, Darlings."

Storie glided toward the back of the house humming and we scurried to close the front door behind us.

Chapter Forty Nine

Timo

"Man, you and Sheila have been red hot since you ate that apple pie. That was two weeks ago, but you still have that fever."

"We've only been on two dates in those two weeks. Nothing to write home about. We're doing everything by the book and, I must confess, it does make things simpler when you're following a basic script but adding some improv along the way."

"Don't downplay it, Dawg. I heard you singing Barry White when you came in last night."

"Timo, you can't penalize a brother for Barry. 'Can't get enough of your love baby?' Classic, bruh."

I blocked the cabinet containing the bowls. "I'm waiting Ricky."

"All we do is talk about ourselves, our goals, and each other until we exhaust the issue. You satisfied?"

I scooted aside. "Uh-huh. We'll see. Meanwhile, who ate all the Fruit Loops?"

"Probably Luke. He came by before I left yesterday afternoon to talk about getting back with Eljay's mom."

"What? Luke's trying to grow up?"

"He's thinking about it. I'm the only one he's mentioned it to."

"D doesn't know? And why you?"

"He said D is still too wounded to talk about commitment without blasting off. Luke wanted somebody who would give him the pros and cons."

I found Apple Jacks in the cupboard. "You're definitely his man if he wants the cons on dating a single mom."

"But Keisha is not any old single mom to Luke. Keisha is Eljay's mom. That's way different."

"Why?"

"Couple of reasons. One, that's his kid. You make 'em, you need to take care of 'em. Period. And two, since Luke's the baby daddy in the situation, there's no baby daddy drama to worry about."

Ricky passed me the milk and I poured. "I feel you. But I hear a lot of gripes from dudes about their kid's mom giving them grief. More than a few cats have told me they got new women to start fresh and have some peace in their lives."

"Too late for that, Timo."

My mouth was full so I couldn't respond.

"I mean, you helped create another human being. You gave up certain options when that happened. Two of them were peace and quiet."

I swallowed hard to get in. "So I'm just trapped with a woman I might not love for eighteen years?"

"Nope. You're in a relationship with the woman that's helping you raise your child for at least eighteen years. Bruh, I'm going to let you in on something. From where I sit, I think brothers ought to be seeing about their kid's mom in addition to helping take care of the kid."

"What? You mean like breaking her off some extra money on top of the child support?"

"Maybe. But I definitely mean being her friend, making sure she's not overly stressed, making sure her car is working right or that everything is fixed around the house."

"Why should I do all that? If I'm not her man anymore, what am I supposed to tell *my* lady and how's my ex's new man going to respond to me being Mr. Fix-It around her house?"

Ricky poured some more cereal. "You tell your lady that you have a child that you love very much who lives with their mom. Because she's doing most of the child rearing, you do everything you can to make sure she has what she needs to do a good job."

"Do you also make conjugal visits?"

"I'm not talking about that. But asking her along if you take your kid to the movies or amusement park won't hurt every now and then."

I grabbed the Apple Jacks for round two. The empty box toyed with my emotions. "How am I supposed to explain dating my ex while I'm dating my new girlfriend?"

"You're not dating your ex. You're making sure the person that is taking care of your child is healthy and happy. The same reason why you're checking on the car or the pipes or the roof or the tennis shoes. If your ex is living foul, how do you think your child will be living? If you have to explain that to your new girlfriend, maybe you shouldn't be with her."

"And what about your ex's new man?"

"He's dating a woman with a child being raised by two parents that are no longer romantically involved. You let him know that while you appreciate the complexity of the arrangement, you're committed to your child and welcome his presence and cooperation. If he's mature enough to understand that children need their father, he'll be alright. If not, maybe mom should find a better man."

"Let's not forget that you're the immature man in the Sheila situation, Ricky."

"Not on that level. I'd have no problem if Steve stepped up and helped Sheila and Diamond. My issue is uncertainty of what he'll do after I enter the picture. I don't need a murder on my rap sheet because he's feeling displaced and becomes all super-aggressive."

"So what did you tell Luke?"

"I told him that, if I were him and still loved Keisha, I'd try to get back with her so our family could be together. But if he was unsure on how he felt about getting back with Keisha right now, just support her and Eljay in an active way and let it develop organically."

I'd poured myself a glass of milk as a consolation prize. Ricky illustrated his point while I wiped my mustache.

"It's like that dude Maurice."

"Maurice Houston?"

"No. Maurice from L.A."

Maurice wore a long braid down his back with black shades and a huge Stevie Wonder grin. "Oh, yeah. What about him?"

"He'd started kicking it with Wanda from College Park last spring and she gave me updates in the teacher's lounge everyday during our planning period. She'd just had a baby and broken it off with the dad during her pregnancy."

"Right. But wasn't Maurice married with a son?"

"Divorced, but yeah. Anyway, one day Wanda comes in complaining about how much time Maurice was spending with his son."

I scratched my neck. "See bruh, you can't win for losing. I thought women wanted men to be good fathers?"

"Well, there's more to it. Turns out that his ex-wife was going deaf and he went over to her place four days a week fixing things and helping his son with homework. Wanda sort of understood, but she felt like the ex-wife was using her disability to hold onto Maurice."

"So what did you tell her?"

"I told Wanda that Maurice wasn't available enough to be in a relationship with her because he was already in a relationship with his family. He made a promise to that lady in sickness and in health. When his son entered the picture, that deepened the vow. A lot of destructive problems in families occur when men try to walk away from their vows just because the romance goes sour. The relationship and vows still exist, no matter what. Lying down with a woman and having a child is a vow to be there and do your part, whether verbal or not."

"Brothers ain't thinking all that when they're getting a cut. You and I weren't."

"You're right. And we were lucky. But with what I know now, my new song is before you lie down with a woman, you'd better be sure you can see yourself married to her and raising kids with her. If you can't, you'd better ask the Lord to give you strength to find your drawers and run out of there before you put something in motion that could bring a lot of pain and suffering to everyone involved."

I frisbeed the empty box toward the garbage can to shift the energy back my way. "Okay, Ann Landers, try this one on for size. What if you have two kids from two different women? What do you do then?"

Ricky deadpanned. "Pick one."

"Which one?"

"I don't know. Hopefully the one you love. Maybe the one you have the most in common with or the one that you could be the best husband to. This might sound crazy, but you could always take them through *The Love Manual* and see who's the best love commitment for you."

I put my cup and bowl in the sink. "You must've eaten that entire pie in one bite. Your picture ought to be on Giovanni's book cover with a caption reading 'Brainwashed Brotha' underneath."

Ricky smirked. "Seriously, I've been tossing around Giovanni's idea that a man would have more success with the system than a woman and I think that would apply to the dude in your scenario. Maybe one of the ladies is truly compatible with him and he wasn't ready while they were together, but now he is."

"What about the other one?"

"She would be a woman that he sees about because he's in relationship with her through his child."

"You're really pushing the boundaries of blended families here, Rick."

"Tell me about it. But it's the best possible world considering the 'multiple baby mama' realities we face in our communities. If the second lady gets married, it will naturally allow the baby daddy to pull back a bit."

"You've got it all figured out. Maybe I should call Giovanni and have her wait to publish the book until you write the chapter for the guys."

Ricky wriggled his fingers. "Maybe you should."

"But I wouldn't buy it unless I knew it worked for the author. So what's it going to be, Ricky? Do you prove the system on Sheila or are you a fraud full of hot air?"

"Our date for this week is already set so I'd have to say that it's the system that's proving itself on me. And you?"

I folded my arms. "As you know, I'm bootlegging my way into an attempted love commitment already in progress."

"Do you not want to see Giovanni happy?"

"Sure I do. Just not with Chester the child molester."

"Well, I hope you know what you're doing because this could backfire big time in your face."

"I'll take my chances."

Chapter Fifty

Gigi

"Hey G, where are you?"

"Pulling off from the office. I'm meeting Eric somewhere in Cabbagetown for lunch."

"Where are you thinking?"

"Maybe *Thumb's Up Diner*. I skipped breakfast and I hear that fish and stone ground grits plate calling me."

"As much as you eat grits, you need to buy stock in Quaker Oats. But I do love that build-your-own-breakfast special. When I want something close to my biscuits and gravy on weekends without the fuss, Princess Di and I catch *Thumb's Up* and it does the trick. Diamond likes the deco block glass in the windows. Gives the place an old-timey feel."

"I chose the Cabbagetown area because it's the midpoint between my office and Emory."

"Gigi, do you have me on speakerphone?"

"Yes, but I'm alone in the car."

"You know I feel like a group of people are sitting there overhearing my deepest secrets."

"Sheila, that's because you used to pick up the phone and listen to your brother's calls."

"Then he started listening to mine and blabbing all my business."

"Good for the goose, Sheila."

"Wait a minute. It's a Wednesday and you're meeting Eric? What's the occasion?"

"Ha, ha. Nothing in particular. Some space opened up in his day and I was free. We decided to go for it."

"About time. I was worried a minute there, Gigi. The man you can only see on the weekend is up to something. But I can call off the assassination team now."

"Girl, you're sick. I mentally kicked Timo in the shin when Eric called me."

"Don't pin it all on Timo. You were dropkicking yourself at the same time."

Sheila was highly skilled at detecting my defenses without dwelling. "But have a good time and eat some catfish for me."

When I arrived, the lunch crowd had scattered so parking and seating came easily. I sat down and ordered, anticipating Eric's arrival. He walked in as the waiter brought my meal. Eric picked the food up off the tray and set it down in front of me. "Your grits, pretty lady."

"Why thank you, kind sir."

"Just a coffee for me. Thanks."

The waiter offered Eric a droll countenance in return and left without response.

"I guess I should've asked before I entered his personal space."

"I guess you should have. If I were you, I'd inspect that Nicaraguan slow roast for floaters."

Eric loosened his tie and touched my hand. "I wish I could stay but I only have time for coffee. I hope you're not upset."

I suppressed my impulse to react because I'd read online that people in the early stages of relationships should never show anger. I tested this theory. "I'm just glad you're here now. How was your day?" I hated myself for making the statement.

"Lousy until I got a call from one of my students that a primary document I've been waiting six weeks to receive landed five minutes ago at Hartsfield. I'm on my way to pick it up."

"Great." I mentally jabbed my own shins with daggers with that one.

The waiter brought the coffee and looked how I felt inside. "Is there anything else?"

He'd divined the words from my mind and rolled them off his lazy tongue. Eric pulled out a twenty and laid it on the tray. "No sir, keep the change."

The tip may have ordinarily excited the heel-worn server, but Eric's lack of attunement extinguished any visible glee. "Y'all have a nice day."

The server clomped away and Eric slid his chair back while sipping his South American beverage.

If I'd kept quiet one second longer, I would've screamed and cracked every glass for miles. "Eric, we need to talk."

Eric lowered his stoop to a seated posture. "Yes, Giovanni?"

I accepted my grits growing cold and breached the argument line. "When we met five years ago, things were amazing. And when you re-entered my life, the fireworks exploded left and right. But I notice that there have been these cooling off periods that I'm having trouble interpreting. Where are you right now? Are you fully committed to making us work?"

Eric pushed his glasses toward the bridge of his nose. "Of course I am. I'm just working so much these days, but I promise to make more time for you when the book is done."

Eric stood while he spoke. "I never told you but your old friend, Timo, showed up in my class a few weeks ago trying to hide in the back. I thought I recognized him then, but knew it for sure when I ran into the hallway to catch a student who had just left a book in my office. When the elevator chimed I saw Timo climbing aboard, making conversation with the same student I was chasing."

I forgot about my grits altogether. "What?"

"I talked with the student later that day, Giovanni. It seems Timo introduced himself as 'Tim' and asked an afternoon full of questions about me, all for selfish reasons no doubt. I admit that I'm preoccupied with work and I'm sorry. But I'm not comfortable with your old boyfriend who poses as your current lover coming to my job and pretending to be a graduate student to spy on me. We can resume this later but it appears that we both have business to handle."

Eric pushed his glasses again and left me speechless in the booth. I pulled out my phone to call Sheila but couldn't before I checked a missed text message: *'Need to talk 2 u 2nite. Straits. My treat.'*

If Timo had been there I would have choked him with those cold grits. I decided to go a step further. I'd embarrass him in a place where his clients were sure to find out about it and drop him like a bucket of bad pork bellies. I hit reply. *Reserve the table for 8. And don't be late.*

Chapter Fifty One

Timo

After I got back from the cleaners, I called Ricky to talk through my ambivalence about being the bearer of bad news. He had just laid things out at his secret rendezvous and awaited Sheila's arrival.

"May I know the location of this week's festivities?"

Ricky has this thing about not letting anybody in on his plans before they've hatched. He's adamant that if somebody other than him knows, then the person he wants to surprise could find out. He claims to keep things under wraps so he won't have to dump my body in the Chattahoochee. All he ever tells are dates, no details.

"It couldn't hurt. I'm at the Galleria."

"The Convention Center? Boy, you must've shelled out a month's pay to get on the inside of that place?"

"I'm not on the inside. I'm outside."

"No A/C and mosquitoes don't mix with women. What's happening out there?"

"This summer, the Galleria is hosting Movies in the Garden."

"I heard of that. They have something like that at Atlantic Station, too."

"Yeah, but A-Station is crowded. Not too many people know about this one. The sponsors provide the movie, popcorn, and bug spray. All you bring are drinks."

"You've been a Fanta man since college, but you might be thinking to go deep into the vineyard for some Tahitian Treat."

Ricky harrumphed. “I’m not Mark Cuban so it won’t be a $90,000 Armand, but I did pick up a nice white wine and two glasses.”

“With popcorn?”

“That and the picnic basket I packed with sandwiches, sliced fruit, and Cracker Jacks in the classic boxes.”

“Not the Cracker Jacks?”

“And you know I couldn’t forget the blanket.”

“Rick, you’re lucky people will be around you two. Otherwise, it might be a long night in the secret garden.”

Ricky sighed. “It might be a long night, anyway. You know tonight’s the night we talk about our hang-ups. I scheduled plenty of time before the movie starts to have that conversation.”

“So, you’re going to tell her about your single mom phobia?”

“I guess so.”

“Bruh, we agreed. You tell Sheila and I tell Giovanni. On the serious tip, I’m not feeling too comfortable with your resolve.”

“I said I’d tell her, Timo.”

“Alright, but I’m going to need some insurance. I’m an investor, not a gambler. If I’m going to jeopardize my chances of ever being with Giovanni because you insisted that I tell her the truth about Eric, then you have to put yourself on the line, too.”

“Insurance like what? Timo, she’ll be here any minute.”

“No problem. Just put your phone on speaker and slip it into your hip case so I can hear.”

“What if you cough or somebody around you starts talking? She’s going to think I’m some kind of a pervert.”

“Well, you are a pervert, but you can tell her that later. And to do away with your excuses, I’ll put my phone on mute so she won’t hear a thing from my side.”

I heard an engine noise get closer and then cut off. “She just pulled up man, I gotta go.”

"Look, if you don't put me on speakerphone, I'm not telling Giovanni. I'll just let her get played like she played me and call it a life. Is that what you want Ricky?"

"Giovanni would hate me as much as she hates you."

"And don't forget about Sheila."

The lingering threat in my tone with the backdrop of the clock bells chiming must have done it. Suddenly I heard the sound on his end expand and a snapping noise before he spoke. "I see you made it."

The notes in Sheila's voice were bright and lively. "I did. You really surprised me with this treasure hunt, Ricky. When I saw that envelope under my wiper this morning, I thought it was a party flyer."

Ricky had playful cadence. "What envelope?"

"You know. The one that said 'The Spa on Paces, 2pm'."

"Did you go?"

Sheila's answer was bedroomy. "You know I went, boy."

Ricky stayed cool. "Sit down and tell me about it."

"Well, the concierge must've had a description of my car because, when I drove up, he opened my door and said they'd been expecting me."

"Had you ever been there?"

"No. As a matter of fact, I'd never been to a spa period. I've done manicures and pedicures, but never anything that elaborate. Between work and Diamond, I never took the time for myself."

At this rate, Ricky was racking up enough electoral votes to be the next Player President. I'm glad he couldn't hear me jocking him on my end. I'd never live it down.

Deep-sea Ricky kept reeling. "So he came to the car, then what?"

"Then I took his arm and he led me inside. Ricky, that place is divine. All those rich colors and fragrances, I almost passed out in the lobby. The concierge handed me a piña colada and informed me that everything had been prepaid. He said I wasn't allowed to tip or spend any money. His last words were, 'Whenever I was ready, the ladies would be waiting for me in the first service room."

"Do you like piña coladas?"

"I do. How'd you know?"

"Who says I did? Keep going."

Sheila's laugh was healthy and infectious. "Okay. I peeked into the first service room and two beautiful sisters welcomed me by name. They said that I'd been scheduled for a Ginger Honey Rice body polish followed by a 60-minute deep tissue massage. I was asked to undress and given a robe while soft flute music played from overhead speakers to set the mood."

Sheila said his name like only a southern woman could. "Ricky when those women came back, they scrubbed me so well and got so deep into my tissues, I fell asleep on the table. The next thing I remember, they were sitting me up to paint my fingers and toes. A plate of sliced strawberries and pineapples lay on my left along with a straw and a bottle of spring water. When I tried to give the sisters an appreciation tip, they just smiled and said it's already been taken care of."

Ricky bantered. "That's a beautiful nail color by the way. So how'd you get here?"

Sheila finished. "The concierge put me in my car and handed me another embroidered envelope like the one on my windshield this morning. Inside the note simply said, 'Cobb Galleria. Clock Tower. 6pm'. I was so relaxed, I barely made it here."

"I'm glad you did."

Sheila's face sounded longer. "And I've been calling you all day. You never answered."

Ricky groaned as if he were stretching. "Well, I was taking care of some odds and ends. Seems like you were tied up anyway."

I didn't hear Sheila respond. I listened for hug rustling or lip smacking, but nothing came until Ricky creaked out a throaty, "What's wrong?"

Chapter Fifty Two

Timo

My battery light blinked, but I couldn't hang up. It was like the day Ricky kidnapped the remote and parked the TV on *Lifetime*. At first I wanted to change the channel, but the way they run the end of a movie into the beginning of another had me sitting there six hours straight. I only had about thirty minutes of battery life left.

Sheila had tears in her voice. "Today was precious to me and I honestly felt like the Queen of Zamunda, but all day long I've been fighting coming back down to earth. I'm a single mom with a young daughter and I can't afford to lose myself in a fairytale that can't come true. Does that make sense?"

"I perfectly understand."

"And I know that The Love Commitment procedure says that tonight should be about values and goals, but I really need to know from you what we're doing here."

"You need to know my intentions?"

"Please."

I just shook my head. My boy Ricky had lain his thug thing down so hard that it got him backed into a sink or swim situation. There ought to be a law against Murphy jumping on a man at times like this.

He responded. "Sheila, let me tell you a story."

"Ricky, I'm serious."

"Me, too. But I promise to answer your question."

Ricky paused, then began. "There's this guy I know that everybody considered somewhat of a ladies' man back in college. I admit our crew was rather immature when it came to commitment, but this guy took the cake. He openly dated at least three women at one time and eventually earned an appropriate nickname from the fellas. All this went on until our junior year. That fall, he met a transfer student who had the same major and shared a couple of his classes. They started studying together and, later, taking in an occasional movie. He still dated and she was also seeing somebody, but they were growing closer every day."

"At the end of the spring semester, she broke up with her guy and my friend decided to sever his ties as well. They talked a time or two over the summer break, but were in different cities and couldn't see each other. During this time, he also made up his mind to declare his feelings for her when they returned for their senior year."

Ricky breathed hard but Sheila remained silent.

He cleared his throat. "The next time he saw her she was pregnant. Apparently, she rekindled with her ex over the summer and this led to that. She and the ex got back together, but my friend was still around being supportive and still in love with her, but heartbroken that life happened all over their chance to give it a try. He chalked it up to karma and left town after graduation, but kept in contact to check on her and the baby. As fate would have it, she broke up with the ex and called to let my friend know."

Sheila spoke this time. "Did they get together?"

"No. He never told her he loved her."

"Why not?"

"Because he couldn't get past the idea of being in a situation where another man would have a say in his family."

"Because of the baby?"

"That and wondering if she really wanted the ex boyfriend and scared the best he would ever be is second fiddle."

Sheila moaned. "So what happened to him?"

"He's still single and hasn't dated since."

"Does he still think bad karma is to blame?"

"Hard to say. But regardless, he's changed for the better."

"What happened with her?"

"She eventually married someone else and my friend accepted her and the baby's happiness as the most important thing. He's been over her for a while now."

I almost didn't hear Sheila's next question. "Ricky, was his nickname in college 'Fabio'?"

I didn't hear any breathing from Ricky at all. I screamed at the phone. "Breathe, bruh!"

Ricky breathed. "You knew? How long?"

"A few minutes. But you seemed very in touch with his feelings. That and Timo called you Fabio at Gigi's house."

Laughter and nerves mingled in his response. "Good ole Timo."

Sheila was resolute. "Truthfully, I also saw a lot of myself in your story. But it was my boyfriend that cheated and I found out after the fact that I was pregnant. So you can understand that getting cheated on again or Diamond being disappointed is a constant fear. So I haven't dated or let anyone get close to us since Steve on purpose. Besides, I don't think guys find single moms single enough for their marrying tastes."

Ricky's voice was strong. "You're wrong, Sheila. I find you single and sexy and smart and spiritual and all the other sensational terms that start with 's'."

She tittered. He stayed strong. "What I did today was to show you that you are exactly the kind of woman I've been searching for. I confess, the idea of being in a similar situation to my college nightmare terrified me. But, believe it or not, Timo helped me come to grips with what I was about to lose if I let that keep me from declaring my feelings for you."

I got out of my car and strutted like George Jefferson speaking into the phone. "That's right. Good ole Timo did that."

Even though they couldn't hear me, I was gratified to have said it.

"Sheila, I know I'm skipping some phases but I don't need to know if I'm sure and I don't need time to break off any other relationships."

Ricky said her name. "Sheila Newell, my actions today were to informally declare my intentions to enter into an exclusive relationship with you that moves us steadily toward marriage. I have taken the liberty of writing my intentions down in calligraphy and having them framed this afternoon; despite my phone sporadically ringing throughout the day. And so Sheila, it is I who needs to know what your intentions are with the offer before you."

Sheila's silence returned with a vengeance. It was so palpable I could physically feel it through telephone. I awaited her response before walking into *Straits*. I heard a crackling noise that sounded like Sheila. "Ricky I..."

Silence. The phone was dead. I shrieked and two other patrons passing by sped their approach to the entrance. "Ricky I...what?"

Chapter Fifty Three

Gigi

I pulled up just in time to see Timo walk into *Straits*. It had the best Singaporean cuisine in town and had plates big enough to share. Ludacris owned this location with his partner, Chris Yeo, and we came here quite a bit when we lived together.

Timo's not fooling anybody. Trying to play innocent and get me on familiar ground while sabotaging my relationship. If he thinks I'm going to let him get away with it, he's got another think coming.

I strolled, National Pan-Hellenic style, toward the table. Timo stood and beckoned me into the chair he held.

"Giovanni, thanks for coming."

I nodded.

He pushed my chair and circled around to his seat. "I debated sending the text but something came to my attention that we need to talk about."

"Oh?"

The waiter came to the table with drinks on a tray and a white napkin over his other forearm. "Good evening, ma'am. Here is your margarita. Your Fuji Apple Shrimp will be out shortly. Meanwhile, enjoy. My name is Bryant and I am at your service."

I looked away from Timo because I knew his eyes were locked on me. His attention to detail was impeccable when it came to making sure our dinners were exquisite. When we were together, he'd insisted on planning date nights so I could be catered to in his presence. I missed that but didn't want it from him. Not now.

I took a sip of the margarita. "Good memory."

"How could I forget?"

I sat back. "You were saying?"

Timo's face tightened. If I didn't know better, I'd think he was actually experiencing discomfort. He spoke. "There's no easy way to say this. Eric is cheating."

"With whom? You?"

"I'm serious. There's this girl at his office named Candace and..."

I didn't let him finish. "...And you just happen to know what goes on in his office because...?"

Timo was trapped in the headlights. It was a new look on him. I attacked. "I'll tell you why? Because you're a scumbag who has nothing better to do than snoop around college campuses to fabricate lies."

Timo grabbed his napkin. "I'm not lying."

"Okay, let's see. Did you sit in Eric's class to spy on him?"

"Yeah, but..."

"Did you go up near his office afterwards?"

"Yes."

"Did you have a conversation with one of Eric's students about him in the Union?"

"Giovanni, you've got it all wrong."

"Do I?"

"Yeah. I know things you don't."

"How Timo? Like what? Proof?" I stung him with his previous words.

He tried to shake off his own bout with irony. "Okay. An acquaintance I know talked to a guy that overheard Eric and Candace arguing outside his office late one night. The guy says she's up there three or four nights a week."

Timo reached for my hand. "Has he ever mentioned Candace by name before?"

My hesitation betrayed the answer. Timo resumed. "Giovanni, if this is on the up and up, why hasn't he mentioned her? If she is as close to him as she says she is, and they work together three to four nights a week, why haven't you heard her name?"

Bryant appeared with our dishes and quickly unfolded his serving table. It was enough reprieve for my bearings to return.

"Here we are. Fuji Apple Shrimp for the lady. And, for you sir, the Kung Pao Lollipop Chicken. Is there anything else you require?"

Timo shook his head. I replied. "Yes. I'll need a 'to-go' box."

"Yes ma'am."

Timo waited until Bryant left earshot. "Giovanni, please don't."

"I've decided to take some of Sheila's advice and you just seconded it."

"What's that?"

"She said men need to be courted, too, so I'm going to mosey up to Eric's office and share a plate of shrimp with him. Since you think he's so lonely that he has to chase undergraduates, he should enjoy the company. I'll be sure to tell him you sent your regards and the shrimp."

Timo

Bryant returned with a box and the check. He handed the first to Giovanni. I stared at the bill dumfounded that Murphy had struck twice in one night. If Ricky's evening had ended anywhere near the way mine was headed, he was somewhere nursing a bottle of Heineken.

When she stood to leave, the crinkle of Giovanni's lips told me her last words hadn't been spoken.

She clanked a fork against her glass, drawing the attention of the crowd momentarily away from their ongoing conversations. "Ladies and gentleman, may I have your attention please? This man, Timo

Barnett, claims to be a financial planner for NFL athletes. He invited me here tonight for dinner, but his only plan was to leave without paying the bill. He is a liar and a charlatan who cannot be trusted to tell the truth or handle money. If you know of anyone considering doing business with him, warn them as soon as you can."

The room murmured and a few camera phones flashed. I smiled through clenched teeth. "Giovanni, what are you doing?"

She spoke openly. "I'm throwing your lies back into your face with a little extra for good measure. Eric told me everything. About you, about you spying on him, and about you pretending to be a student and interrogating Candace. I knew I should've never let you get close to me or my chance to have a happy life with a good man. Leave me alone, Timo. Don't call me, don't text me, and stay away from me!"

Giovanni grabbed her purse from the seatback. "Now, if you'll excuse me, I have a dinner date with a grown man who can handle a grown woman."

Giovanni tossed her wrap over her shoulders, grabbed the box, and walked toward the door as if defiantly taking a sobriety test. She stopped at the Maitre d', then continued out to the walkway. The Maitre d' looked at me and nodded. When Bryant brought the credit card receipt over, it had already been signed with one word, 'Timo', and a 50% gratuity added to the total.

Without protest, I retrieved my card and staggered to the parking lot. Giovanni was long gone and my phone battery was still dead. So were my chances of ever getting her back.

Chapter Fifty Four

Gigi

My gait was brisk in the warm night air. The posts and hanging chains kept sentry over me on the lawn in front of Eric's building. I'd heard him talk about Candler Library, but I didn't realize that it was virtually at the center of campus. That would've been fine if I'd worn my walking shoes. But because of my four inch heels, my admiration for the Spanish roof tile and the original marble foyer was severely abbreviated.

Sheila hadn't returned any of my calls all day. After meeting Eric, I planned to track her down but I knew between work, Diamond, and Ricky that Sheila had her hands full. I left her a voicemail on the way over; however, I doubt if she could unscramble the gibberish I recorded. How dare Timo interfere in my private life? I was breathing through my ears trying to calm down before I reached Eric. The worst thing I could do was bring Timo in there strapped to my back after the Diner scene earlier today.

Once in the lobby, I slipped off my pumps and gave my back and leg tendons a much needed rest. To my right was a bank of elevators, but that would've spoiled the surprise. So I opted to climb the central staircase to the fourth floor and admire the architecture of the building on my way up. Flanking the enormous corridor entrances were sets of plaster columns carved with ornate floral designs that would have fit perfectly into an ancient Pharaoh's burial chamber. The scent of the shrimp wafted upwards and filled the space. I prayed that the fragrance didn't give me away.

I reached the fourth floor and scrolled down the wall directory. It designated Eric's office as 407 and the placard posted on the adjacent door read 415. I turned left and tiptoed with my shoes and shrimp in hand. I heard voices but couldn't make out what was being said. The office numbers continued to descend, so I inched farther down, drawing closer to the voices as well.

A woman's tone was commanding. "Eric, I can't do this."

Eric? Even if Timo was right about Eric working late with his assistant, the familiarity in her tone stopped me mid-stride.

Eric responded. "Candace, you can't leave me now. I need you."

"You're not even focused on what we're doing. Your mind is on your new girlfriend. Surprised? You think I didn't know about her, Eric?"

"What does Giovanni have to do with you and me?"

I couldn't believe my ears. My heart was telling me to back up, but anger willed my feet forward. I turned my ear toward the light to concentrate."

"Candace, this is our baby. You can't just take it from me now. Not after all this time."

"Oh, yes I can. Watch me."

The emotion in the room grew intense. I could feel my own breath bouncing off the doorframe.

Eric's pitch lowered. "Candace, I know you can do this by yourself, but I'm right here. Once you cool off, I think you'll realize that it should have my name, too."

Eric sniffed the air and located the aroma with his nose. The young woman next to him followed his eyes to the styrofoam box, shoes, and the face of the hands that held them.

Timo

There were no back roads to make up the time. Even though Ponce de Leon was clear, Briarcliff is a toss-up anytime, day or night. But once I hit North Decatur Road, I was there in no time flat.

Since getting my new phone, I hadn't yet purchased a car charger so I couldn't pick Ricky's brain on recent events. He might've hit a homerun and be watching a movie on a blanket with Sheila or he might've struck out and be watching grass grow by himself. Either way, he may not be up to talking but I could have at least sent him a text to keep him posted. My immediate lack of options made his example about kids taking away certain choices pop out in 3D.

I spotted Giovanni's Benz but decided to use the back lot, just in case she was still angry when she came out. With my track record tonight, I'd be lucky if she didn't have dynamite and a detonator in store for the grand finale. Full sprint, I sliced into the doorway as a student exited. The desk attendant raised a finger to protest, but put it down in futility once I whizzed by. The smell of apples had created a sweet and sour trail that faded when I left the general area and dipped into an open elevator.

I pushed the button and paced back and forth, rubbing my head. "What am I doing?"

Was this crazy love? It had to be. Because I felt like the biggest fool in town; chasing a woman that wanted another man and hated my guts. By the time this was over, I'd have no clients and no woman. Still I was driven to tell her how I felt, come what may.

When the elevator door separated, I heard Giovanni's voice echoing into the hallway. "You know Eric, I felt terrible when you came over and found Timo at my house. I didn't know what you thought of me, but I knew it couldn't have been good. I agonized over it for days afterward until I said to myself, 'If he cared enough to find me after all these years, then things will be fine.' But that's before I knew that you were one of those teachers who takes advantage of your position and seduces your students."

She believed me? As I pondered the question, I volleyed between excitement and disbelief. I never would've imagined in a million years that she'd actually accepted what I'd told her earlier. But why would she say that stuff about me being a liar? Not enough information. I inched on tippy toes.

Another woman laughed in the room. "Is this her, Eric? You're choosing *this* over what we have?"

Candace? I knew it had to be, but this was bonkers. Mr. Perfect was caught in his web of lies, and Giovanni had to endure the pain his double-life inflicted. I clinched my fist, set my jaw line, and listened for the right moment to pounce.

Eric's voice grew twitchy. "Candace, Giovanni. This is all a big misunderstanding. I can explain."

Giovanni cut in. "Explain what, Eric? I heard it all and I see your baby's mama right here."

That one stunned me. I craned my neck and tried not to shuffle my feet.

Eric responded. "My what? Look, just sit down and we can straighten this out."

Giovanni exploded. "Don't tell me what to do Eric. I should bathe you with these Fuji Shrimp, but they're too good to waste on a turd like you!"

Candace tagged in. "You said it sister. We can definitely agree there. And just to set the record straight, Eric is not my man. For lack of a better term, he's my protégé."

Her dramatic pause met no resistance from Eric. Candace continued. "You see, for the last two years I've been trying to publish my work in the field but, because I'm an undergraduate, no respectable journals or academic publishers would touch me. I received three rejection letters from major presses that practically accused me of stealing some unknown scholar's work. When I showed the letters to Eric, he said he had a way we could help each other."

Eric pleaded. "Giovanni, she's lying. Don't listen to her."

Giovanni's silence and my mental hunger overpowered Eric's helpless appeal.

Candace resumed. "So I gave him my essays for comments and a few edits. He revised and submitted them to top-tier journals listing himself as primary author. When the first one got accepted, he did it four more times with the same result."

Giovanni questioned. "So you let him take credit for your work?"

"Believe it or not, it happens all the time in college. Students do the research and professors stick their name on it as first author. What can you do until you get your work out there? All I'd get was billing as second author, but at least my name and work would be in the literature. So, yes, I let it happen. And now that I've been recognized in peer-reviewed journals, it's a different ballgame. When that guy came around asking about Eric, the reason I knew the titles and content of all his publications is because I wrote them. I also knew that guy wasn't familiar with the field. Your friend, Tim or whatever his name is, knew his finance. A little weak on his fiscal policy and global economics but, he was cute so I drank his soda and answered his questions.

Candace had struck me as incredibly smart and insightful during our conversation. Obviously I didn't know how smart.

Giovanni flowed with her. "So what was all the talk about 'our baby' coming from Eric a minute ago?"

"Oh, that. What lover boy has been trying to conceal from you and everyone else is the book I'm writing that he's trying to steal and put his name on. That's what he calls 'our baby'."

Eric erupted. "That's a lie!"

Candace spoke in a forceful monotone. "Eric, sit down or I will file a plagiarism complaint with the Dean in the morning."

No words from Eric, just a dull thud and Candace began again.

"Eric is good as an editor, footnote locator, and someone to bounce ideas off, but he's not an original thinker. He knows that so we worked well together until he got distracted recently with you. I admit I was jealous, but jealous of the time your relationship was taking from the completion of my book. However, it did give me time to think of a solution."

Giovanni relaxed. "And what was that?"

"I decided that Eric had outgrown his usefulness and, since he's already been handsomely compensated with a group of publications he could have never written on his own, I had the power and moral authority to end our arrangement. He sensed my growing dissatisfaction. That's why he broke your lunch date today to fetch that manuscript. To appease me. Now that I have it, I don't need him anymore."

Panic flooded Eric. "But Candace you can't do this to me. I deserve credit for my contribution. I'm up for early tenure in September. If you publish that book by yourself, it'll ruin me."

Candace rejoined. "You used me, I used you. We helped each other. However you want to see it, it's over. I'm out of here."

That heightened anxiety returned to Eric's voice. "I won't let you do it!"

Candace screamed. I sprang past Giovanni and leapt onto Eric like we were in a UFC title fight. As a reflex, he released Candace and tried to protect his facial region from the judgment I rained down upon him. I was no B.B. King, but I served Eric a heaping helping of the blues that night.

It was only Giovanni's voice that stopped the destruction. "No, Timo!"

She had her arms around my waist with her head burrowed into my back. I turned to put my arms around her and walked her out. Candace stood in the doorway with a pouch under her arm. "Girlfriend, Eric didn't cheat on you, but he's a liar on levels much deeper than that. Now I'm not sure where you stand, but from over here, the brother you're holding is the man you need to be with."

Giovanni pulled her head from my chest and asked. "How old are you?"

Candace struck a pose. "Twenty-one and loving it. You never had any worries on my end. Underneath that con-artist exterior, Eric was too geeky for me. Besides, I've got my eye on this beefcake named Pearl. Now there's a rugged intellect if I ever saw one."

I gave her a wink and she shot me the peace sign. "Deuces."

Candace meandered over to the elevator and pressed the down button. Giovanni and I squeezed each other until the stairwell entrance swallowed us. We continued that way down all four flights. Eric moaned, but never emerged from his office.

Chapter Fifty Five

Gigi

We walked down all four flights in silence. I'd cry, Timo would pull me close. Then I'd sniffle, dry my eyes and pull away. This happened until we reached the landing. I broke away from him and ran past the seated attendant through the Corinthian columns and onto the walkway. Timo jogged behind me, waiting for me to reach my limit. He didn't have to wait long.

I kept walking with my heels and box still in hand. Timo's footsteps were audible, but he didn't say a word all the way to my car. I placed the shoes and box on the roof and began to pelt Timo with the base of my fists. "Why Timo? Why?"

Timo smothered me in his arms. "I don't know why, Baby. The guy's a jerk."

"Not him. You? Why you? Why now?"

Timo held my face in his hands searching for meaning.

"Why are you so perfect now that I've accepted that we don't want the same things?"

"Giovanni, I'm not perfect. But there's one thing I'm sure about… that I love you. I did feel like there was something off about Eric and I wanted to expose that to get back at you for dismissing me, but those things faded. The real reason I did all of this—following him and following you tonight—is because I'm willing to do whatever it takes to show you that I'm ready."

A lone tear dropped from my eye. "Timo, how can I really know you're serious?"

"Because remember how you took me near Lake Lanier and told me you always wanted a wedding in a small, natural setting?"

I lifted my head. "All that time I thought you weren't listening."

"Well, I was. And I spoke with the caretaker of that Bamboo Garden and reserved it for us. I also visited your parents today to share my plans and they gave me their blessing."

My system was on overload. "You drove to Tuskegee?"

Timo nodded.

"And spoke to my parents?"

"I did. Had a long talk with your dad, too. We went by Mr. Ford's Barber Shop and I met all the people that knew you when. Everyone is on standby for the next six months."

I refused to let myself hope. "Timo, be as clear as you can. What are you saying to me?"

Timo caressed my left hand. "Giovanni, we were together for three years and apart for the same. But in my heart, there's been no other woman but you for all six. We have experienced all the phases together except one."

Timo went down on his right knee and brought his hand from behind his back. The black velvet sparkled in the moonlight. He opened it with his fingers. "Giovanni, I was scared three years ago the night you asked me where we were headed. Baby, I 'm not scared anymore. I love you and need you in my life. And, if you will have me, it would give me great joy for you to be my wife."

I love you because it's been so good for so long that if I didn't love you I'd have to be born again. I bent down and stroked his cheek and kissed him slowly. "Timo, I'm overwhelmed by this moment and have to let you know that I do love you, never stopped. Still, I won't allow myself to say 'yes' to you. But I am willing to skip you up to the Verification Phase so I can spend some time getting to know you all over again."

Crouched there, Timo opened my palm with his thumb and

placed the box in my hand. "I may need this in a few months, so could you keep it safe for me until then?"

I nodded and we ended the night in the in the campus observatory, gazing at stars, finishing the shrimp and lollipop chicken dinner we never started, and working toward a bona fide love commitment.

Timo

Giovanni was breathtaking. Our wedding party was small, just Ricky and Sheila on either side. Diamond dropped multicolored rose petals to represent our past, present, and future together. Others in attendance were Giovanni's family, Sheila and Ricky's parents, D.C., Luke, Keisha, Eljay, and various friends from far and near. As part of the ceremony, those who chose spoke a blessing over our union, surrounded, and prayed for us before we took our vows. After jumping the broom, we shifted to a covered tent housing the reception. I knew Muhmaw was smiling down on her grandbaby and pleased that I had more family to love and be loved by.

While Giovanni danced with her father, I reminisced on how much had happened with the crew in the last six months. *The Love Manual* has sold 100,000 copies in Atlanta alone and is still going strong across the country. Giovanni has been a guest on dozens of talk shows, radio broadcasts, and internet podcasts heard around the world. **Th**e**L**ove**C**ommitment.com has had ten million hits to date and 500,000 people receive weekly emails as well as advice on specific love commitment situations. Love Commitment Reading Circles and Relationship Groups were being created globally and, more importantly, Sheila received daily emails from men and women reporting freshly declared love commitments.

By the goo-goo eyes and the rock on Sheila's finger, you can guess what happened with her and Ricky that night my phone died. Luke hasn't made it official yet, but he and Keisha started dating again and working through *The Love Manual*. Giovanni did incorporate many of Ricky's suggestions and and eventually asked him to co-author the portion of the book for guys. D.C. was still single, but vibing mighty hard with Mona by Aunt Patty's punch near the dessert table. If he showed up at *Applebee's* anytime during the next week, we'd be planning his bachelor's party in the next twelve months for sure.

Our bags were packed and waiting in the limousine. It was December, two days after Giovanni's birthday, and she was courageous enough to let me surprise her for our honeymoon destination. I chose The Turks and Caicos Islands for their coral reefs, white sandy beaches, and crystal turquoise waters. Giovanni loved to snorkel and, once we boarded the plane, it'd be only a three-hour flight from Atlanta to Grand Turk Island. During that time of year, herds of humpback whales pass near the shores and the vibration of their song can be felt while swimming or diving.

Not much was happening in my line of business during the holidays, but Giovanni had to hire a staff to run Georgian Realty while she focused on incorporating what she'd learned into Love Commitment seminars for churches, colleges, and public forums. The only real estate clients she insisted on personally representing were Storie and Walters Killingsworth.

Ricky tapped his watch and grabbed the microphone. "Everyone, my last duty as best man is to make sure that these two lovebirds make it to the airport for their secret honeymoon vacation spot known to everyone except Giovanni."

My wife made a face. The crowd applauded and formed a soul-train line which we danced from the head table to the open limo door.

Ricky and Sheila met us there. He spoke first. "Whoever thought you'd be first, Timo? We're all following your lead, brother. Much love and success to you both."

Sheila echoed the sentiment. "G, I'm so happy for you. You've been my best friend since day one and I love you with all my heart. Timo, you're my brother now so you two take care of each other and take my love wherever you go. Now get in that car before you spend your honeymoon stuck in game day traffic."

We all exchanged goodbyes. I kissed Sheila on the cheek and, this time, Ricky and I gave each other full body hugs. We knew it was a new era and somehow the love between us as men had to become deeper and more transparent.

When the ladies released their embrace, I helped Giovanni into the backseat and we embarked on our new journey.

I breathed first. "We really did it."

"Yes, we did."

"Giovanni, so let me ask you, what's the next phase after marriage?"

"I guess it's having a good marriage. But we'll need a little more experience before we can write that one."

"Correct as always. By the way, thank you."

"For what?"

"For making me the happiest man alive today."

Giovanni blushed as her purse vibrated. It had been in the car during the ceremony and reception. She put it on speaker so I could hear.

"Hello? Storie?"

"Hi Giovanni. How are you, Dear?"

"I'm wonderful. Guess what? Today is my wedding day so your great, great grandmother's work is still enriching our lives."

"Giovanni, Walters and I are elated for you. Please forgive this intrusion on your special day and do convey our congratulations to your husband."

"I will. But you're not bothering us. We're on our way to the airport. What's up?"

"I have great news. Just this morning we were contacted by a cash buyer who is leaving the country tonight but wanted to come by and close the deal this afternoon. We were in the area and called our attorney to draw up the paperwork and meet us at the house. Everyone is here now but we need you to come sign for your commission check. After all, you are our agent."

Giovanni looked to me, doing a silent end zone celebration in her wedding heels. "Do we have time?"

I gestured. "We'll make time. Storie your neighborhood is along the way. We'll be there in ten minutes."

Giovanni gave the driver their address and we were off.

He exited the interstate, made a few turns, and we were there in eight minutes flat. The driver opened her door. Giovanni looked back. "You coming?"

I reached for the refrigerator door. "No, I'm going to utilize the comforts of this limo while we still have it. You go ahead and enjoy your moment."

Giovanni leaned over to kiss me, lifted her hemline, and stepped out of the limo. A tall, fiftyish brother met her at the steps and escorted her across the threshold.

Inside, Storie embraced her. "Giovanni, you know Walters. Allow me to introduce our attorney and friend, Anderson McClain."

"How do you do, Mr. McClain?"

The fit, older gentleman rose from behind the stack of documents and took Giovanni's hand. "Super, but I'll get better. Salutations to you and your new husband."

"Thank you."

Storie held Giovanni's train and guided her to the closing table. "It appears that we are all here."

Giovanni surveyed the faces again and inquired. "Where's the buyer?"

Storie's laugh infected the entire room. "My Dear, he's right behind you."

Giovanni whirled and beheld me standing in the entrance.

She giggled then tilted her head. "I don't understand."

Mr. McClain beckoned to me. "Right this way, sir. We have simplified things so you will only need to sign here, here, and here."

Giovanni came to my side, whisper shouting. "Timo, what's going on? This is a 3.3 million dollar house. We can't afford this."

"I know. But Storie made me promise to let her explain it to you so...Storie?"

Giovanni swiveled to Storie's pleasant expression. "Giovanni, two months ago we received an invitation from your fiancé to your wedding. Walters called to convey our gratitude and Timo asked if he could meet with us during our next visit to town to discuss marriage and thank us for helping you. So we asked him to meet us here for tea and pastries a few weeks ago. But an amazing thing happened. As we talked, Walters and I watched how he responded to the house and, more importantly, how the house responded to him. He didn't have your knowledge of the décor and furnishings, but the house called to him and entreated him, much like it did you on your first visit."

I signed the paperwork and alleviated some of Giovanni's confusion. "So Walters and Storie sat me down in the parlor and told me that the house had chosen us as its new owners. They said this was not a financial transaction, but there were associated fees that could not be avoided."

Giovanni huffed. "Like 3.3 million dollars?"

I replied. "No. Like two hundred thousand dollars."

Giovanni's confusion returned. I continued. "Well with my savings and the draft picks I'd just signed, I had exactly two hundred thousand in the bank. Storie and Walters said we could have the house if I agreed to bring a cashiers' check for two hundred thousand dollars to pay their agent the commission owed."

Giovanni covered her mouth. Mr. McClain motioned with his pen.

"Giovanni, if you will sign here, here, here, and here our business is complete and you can see Mr. Barnett for your remuneration."

I pulled an envelope from my breast pocket and handed it to Giovanni. She opened it and the tears started to flow while speaking to Walters and Storie. "I don't know what to say. Thank you doesn't seem like enough."

Mr. McClain waved goodbye and Walters handed Giovanni a ring of keys. "Happy birthday Giovanni, and congratulations to you both. Care for each other the way we know you will care for the house."

I answered. "We will, sir. Thank you for everything."

Storie and Giovanni had a lingering hug. Then Walters and Storie grabbed our hands a prayed a blessing for our marriage and our new home.

We said our farewells then watched Storie and Walters drive away. After locking the door, I turned to find Giovanni two inches from me. I chuckled. "Giovanni, are you alright?"

"Not really. Timo, you messed me up with that one. I was trying to be all sensible with this love thing, but you've made that impossible now. So I'm going to need two favors from you."

"What's that?"

Giovanni put her arms around my waist. "Since you've totally crossed over into friend territory with your thoughtfulness, I need you to start calling me Gigi."

I welled up inside and nodded. "And the second?"

"The second is easy. After we get back into the limo, arrive at the airport, and touchdown in Turks and Caicos...I'm going to need your help releasing some oxytocin."

Afterword

Dear Reader:

I sincerely hope you enjoyed your Love Commitment journey as much as I enjoyed writing it. Anyone acquainted with the greater Atlanta area and all it has to offer will recognize many familiar landmarks. Whether you are or not, the next time you visit Atlanta, I encourage you to search out all the locations named because they are all real. But I'll let you in on a secret: this book is only the beginning. **T**he **L**ove **C**ommitment is a real-life system contained in a real-life book called *The Love Manual*. And if you haven't yet visited the site, www.**T**he**L**ove-**C**ommitment.com, when you do you'll discover that it is real, too.

Being in strong, committed relationships that lead to marriage is not magic. Instead it's more like science, social-science, but we need to know the rules of the system. Now, you can learn the rules by yourself. However, to implement the system, it's best if the people in your relationship-environment are on the same page. Getting them there is easy if you follow these steps:

(1) Tell everyone you know how much you enjoyed this book and send them to the website to purchase a copy, learn more about **TLC**, and become a subscriber to our free weekly relationship articles and advice column.

(2) Organize **TLC** Reading Circles where you come together and discuss this novel and the inner world of the characters using the "Reading Circle" questions provided on the following pages. If you are already a member of a book club or looking to start your own, this is a perfect opportunity. Do this as many times and with as many circles as you like.

(3) Those who are interested in pursuing these themes on a personal level should begin a **TLC** Relationship Group that would start by discussing the "Relationship Group" questions provided on the following pages. Unlike the "Reading Circle" questions, the "Relationship Group" questions look at you and your readiness to form a Love Commitment.

(4) The next step for the Relationship Group is to order *The Love Manual* (www.TheLoveCommitment.com) and come together to discuss the various phases of **T**he **L**ove **C**ommitment process. Guidelines to facilitate this are found within *The Love Manual*. As you do, you will begin to evaluate your romantic interactions according to The Love Commitment model and, eventually, establish healthy relationships with the intention of being married in the time you specify. Please note that, although they can be, neither the Reading Circle nor the Relationship Group is gender-specific so women and men can both participate if you wish. Some of you may even end up getting married.

(5) The last step is for the Relationship Groups to be a source of encouragement and support for members in young relationships. It's a place where you can celebrate triumphs when moving from phase to phase, or a place where you can (at your discretion) have a sounding-board to work through "Decision Moments" as well as share your feelings after a love interest

does not work out. Anytime a member has a triumph, forms a Love Commitment by getting engaged, or ultimately gets married, throw a Love Commitment Party that celebrates the couple and announces the good news to the community.

In our lifetime, we will have families, children and marriages that are strong and will thrive for generations to come. But we must do it together. *TheLoveCommitment.com* and *The Love Manual* are the first steps. They get you to the altar. Cultivating a young marriage will be covered next time you see Gigi, Timo, Sheila, and Ricky. Until then, I wish you Love and Commitment in all that you do.

ds

Reading Circle/ Book Club Questions

(1) What was the central theme of the novel and what are the various levels on which it unfolded?

(2) Compare and contrast the relationships of Gigi and Timo vs. Sheila and Ricky. In what ways did their past both prevent and prepare them to meet the challenges they respectively faced?

(3) Walters did not say much throughout the narrative. Did his character have any impact and, if so, what was his contribution?

(4) Discuss the role of the guy group (Timo, Ricky, Luke, and D.C.) and whether they helped or hindered the formation of the eventual Love Commitments.

(5) From what you read about The Love Commitment system, what do you understand it to be and do you believe it will work? If not, what would need to be changed to make it work?

(6) Were Sheila's fears of men not being interested in single mothers irrational or well-founded?

(7) Were Ricky's hang-ups on dating and marrying a woman with children reasonable, unreasonable, immature, stubborn, hypocritical, too particular, or some combination of these?

(8) What was the function of the Grant Park House in the narrative and what did it reflect in each person it encountered?

(9) Eric did not cheat on Gigi with Candace. Did Gigi discard their relationship too hastily?

(10) Do you think Timo really loved Gigi or was the presence of competition the catalyst for him to step up his game? Would it be acceptable if that were his reason?

(11) Is Ricky's position that the non-resident father should attend to both the needs of his child and the non-romantic needs of his child's mother feasible or appropriate? What in Ricky's character or his past might motivate that kind of response from him?

(12) Did Timo's upbringing play a part in the way he viewed and treated women?

(13) How did Storie function in the narrative? Does her relationship with Walters seem unrealistic or is it governed by a different set of rules?

(14) How would you characterize Candace? Was she strong, fierce, manipulative, heartless, shrewd, honest, dishonest, driven, or some combination of these?

(15) By the end of the novel, did you have a feeling of closure about the plot and the various societal issues raised? If not, discuss some of the unresolved themes that nag or trouble you.

Relationship Group Questions

(1) With which character do you identify most and why? If it is a combination of characters, which ones and which attributes of each do you possess? Do you recognize other characters as people currently or previously in your life?

(2) Gigi and Timo dated for three years with mixed intentions. What were the length and circumstances of your longest adult relationship that did not lead to marriage?

(3) Are you ready right now to be in a committed relationship that leads to marriage in two years or less? If so or not, why?

(4) Sheila and Luke both had children from previous relationships. Do you have children from a previous relationship and would you consider marrying someone who does? Why or why not?

(5) How would you describe yourself and how would other people describe you? Are the two descriptions similar or different?

(6) Do you have goals for the next one, three, and five years? If so, what are they and do they include marriage and children?

Are these goals written in a visible place that can be reviewed daily?

(7) Consider Sheila's original stance on Humanities Majors. How important is financial standing in your mate selection process? Does the person need to make more money than you or would you work toward marriage with someone who made much less than you or who was unemployed? Is the answer different for women vs. men?

(8) Are you the type of person you would date and marry in two years or less? What areas would you need to spruce up before you would date and marry yourself?

(9) Is three to six months too soon to tell a love interest that you'd like to date exclusively with the intention of working toward marriage?

(10) Do you understand the non-religious rationale for the 'no sex until marriage' clause? Could you personally abide by this or would you opt for Plan B—the 'no sex until a Love Commitment (i.e. public engagement) is established'?

(11) List the ten most desirable traits of your ideal mate. Then scratch off seven that you would be willing to sacrifice if you could have the top three.

(12) Beyond money, what would it take to have a marriage like Walters and Storie? Can you name three couples (that you know personally) who have a marriage of comparable caliber? Two? One?

(13) Did you grow up in an environment where marriage was the norm or the exception? Are most of your friends married or single? Do you think these environmental factors have any influence (positively or negatively) on your feelings about relationships, the quality of your relationships, or your current marital status?

(14) Do you believe that other men and women (like yourself) would respect The Love Commitment system if exposed to it? Would you be willing to talk to one new person each day about The Love Commitment phases to spread the concept?

(15) Are you ready and willing to join TheLoveCommitment.com online community, receive access to free weekly articles and advice columns, order *The Love Manual*, as well as learn and stick with the principles of The Love Commitment system until you and your Relationship Group find the marital happiness you seek? Even after you are married, would you still be willing to teach the system and its principles to friends, family, and other singles looking to be married?

(Hint: The only way to learn The Love Commitment system is to secure a copy of *The Love Manual*. Since it is partially a workbook that you will write in, everyone will need their own copy.)

About the Author

Darryl "Doc" Scriven is a graduate of both Florida A&M University and Purdue University. He earned a Ph.D. in Philosophy and has taught at Wilberforce University, Southern University, Tuskegee University, and lectured at dozens of universities across the country and world. Doc is the author of seven books ranging from fiction to academic to self-improvement. ***TheLoveCommitment.com*** is his second novel. He is co-founder of The African American Family Enrichment Institute in Atlanta, Georgia and, as such, is committed to building families that will thrive for generations. To find out when Doc will be speaking in your area, to host a Love Commitment Seminar for your group, or to obtain special discounts on bulk orders of this book and *The Love Manual*, visit www.TheLoveCommitment.com for details.

www.ingramcontent.com/pod-product-compliance
Lightning Source LLC
LaVergne TN
LVHW091044080826
845145LV00002B/623

* 9 7 8 0 9 8 2 7 4 3 2 1 8 *